Readers love
ANDREW GREY

Borrowed Heart

"…Grey's breezy style makes it all go down smoothly. Fans of destination romances will find this one perfectly fits the bill."
—Publishers Weekly

"All in all, *Borrowed Heart* was a delightful mix of heavy-hitting personal issues and fluffy happily ever after story telling."
—Joyfully Jay

Rebound

"I just found so much joy in these characters and I loved getting to know them."
—Diverse Reader

"This book was a great read with a huge air of mystery and some danger about it."
—Gay Book Reviews

Unfamiliar Waters

"It is engaging and sweet with imperfect guys adding to the appeal. The tension and mystery providing the stage that allows the romance to bloom."
—Kimmers' Erotic Book Banter

"This story is such a lovely, intriguing story… the blooming romance is oh so sweet and lifts our hearts in expectation…."
—TTC Books and More

More praise for
ANDREW GREY

The Best Worst Honeymoon Ever

"…in his usual deft manner, Grey leads the reader through it all and still leaves that sense of romance and hope that seem to follow in all his books. This is a great and fun summer read."

—Paranormal Romance Guild

"…if you're looking for a read full of gentle loving, great scenery, amazing excursions and wildlife, and a perfect happy ending, then you will probably love this novel as much as I do."

—Rainbow Book Reviews

New Tricks

"I strongly suggest you get a copy, a cup of your favorite drink, a nice snuggly place to curl up and lose yourself in a wonderful world Andrew Greys making!"

—Love Bytes

"Another simply lovely heartwarming story by Andrew Grey."

—Open Skye Books

Reunited

"Sweet... it was a relaxing 20 minute read..."

—Gay Book Reviews

"Cute second chance at love story with a high school reunion turning into an unlikely first date."

—Open Skye Book Reviews

By ANDREW GREY

Accompanied by a Waltz
All for You
Between Loathing and Love
Borrowed Heart
Buried Passions
Chasing the Dream
Crossing Divides
Dominant Chord
Dutch Treat
Eastern Cowboy
In Search of a Story
New Tricks
Noble Intentions
North to the Future
One Good Deed
On Shaky Ground
The Playmaker
Rebound
Reunited
Running to You
Saving Faithless Creek
Shared Revelations
Survive and Conquer
Three Fates
To Have, Hold, and Let Go
Turning the Page
Unfamiliar Waters
Whipped Cream

ART
Legal Artistry • Artistic Appeal
Artistic Pursuits • Legal Tender

BOTTLED UP
The Best Revenge • Bottled Up
Uncorked • An Unexpected Vintage

BRONCO'S BOYS
Inside Out • Upside Down
Backward • Round and Round
Over and Back

THE BULLRIDERS
A Wild Ride • A Daring Ride
A Courageous Ride

BY FIRE
Redemption by Fire
Strengthened by Fire
Burnished by Fire • Heat Under Fire

CARLISLE COPS
Fire and Water • Fire and Ice
Fire and Rain
Fire and Snow • Fire and Hail
Fire and Fog

CARLISLE DEPUTIES
Fire and Flint • Fire and Granite
Fire and Agate • Fire and Obsidian

CHEMISTRY
Organic Chemistry • Biochemistry
Electrochemistry
Chemistry Anthology

DREAMSPUN DESIRES
#4 – The Lone Rancher
#28 – Poppy's Secret
#60 – The Best Worst Honeymoon Ever

EYES OF LOVE
Eyes Only for Me • Eyes Only for You

FOREVER YOURS
Can't Live Without You • Never Let
You Go

GOOD FIGHT
The Good Fight • The Fight Within
The Fight for Identity
Takoda and Horse

Published by DREAMSPINNER PRESS
www.dreamspinnerpress.com

By ANDREW GREY (CONT.)

HEARTS ENTWINED
Heart Unseen • Heart Unheard
Heart Untouched

HOLIDAY STORIES
Copping a Sweetest Day Feel
Cruise for Christmas
A Lion in Tails
Mariah the Christmas Moose
A Present in Swaddling Clothes
Simple Gifts
Snowbound in Nowhere • Stardust

LAS VEGAS ESCORTS
The Price • The Gift

LOVE MEANS…
Love Means… No Shame
Love Means… Courage
Love Means… No Boundaries
Love Means… Freedom
Love Means … No Fear
Love Means… Healing
Love Means… Family
Love Means… Renewal
Love Means… No Limits
Love Means… Patience
Love Means… Endurance

LOVE'S CHARTER
Setting the Hook • Ebb and Flow

PLANTING DREAMS
Planting His Dream
Growing His Dream

REKINDLED FLAME
Rekindled Flame • Cleansing Flame
Smoldering Flame

SENSES
Love Comes Silently
Love Comes in Darkness
Love Comes Home
Love Comes Around
Love Comes Unheard
Love Comes to Light

SEVEN DAYS
Seven Days • Unconditional Love

STORIES FROM THE RANGE
A Shared Range • A Troubled Range
n Unsettled Range
A Foreign Range • An Isolated Range
A Volatile Range • A Chaotic Range

STRANDED
Stranded • Taken

TALES FROM KANSAS
Dumped in Oz • Stuck in Oz
Trapped in Oz

TALES FROM ST. GILES
Taming the Beast
Redeeming the Stepbrother

TASTE OF LOVE
A Taste of Love • A Serving of Love
A Helping of Love • A Slice of Love

WITHOUT BORDERS
A Heart Without Borders
A Spirit Without Borders

WORK OUT
Spot Me • Pump Me Up • Core Training
Crunch Time • Positive Resistance
Personal Training
Cardio Conditioning
Work Me Out Anthology

Published by DREAMSPINNER PRESS
www.dreamspinnerpress.com

ANDREW GREY
SURVIVE
AND CONQUER

Mandy
I hope you love
it! Hugs

DREAMSPINNER
PRESS

Andrew Grey

Published by

DREAMSPINNER PRESS

5032 Capital Circle SW, Suite 2, PMB# 279, Tallahassee, FL 32305-7886 USA
www.dreamspinnerpress.com

Survive and Conquer
© 2019 Andrew Grey

Cover Art
© 2019 Kanaxa
Cover content is for illustrative purposes only and any person depicted on the cover is a model.

Trade Paperback ISBN: 978-1-64405-456-7
Digital ISBN: 978-1-64405-455-0
Library of Congress Control Number: 2019934511
Trade Paperback published July 2019
v. 1.0

Printed in the United States of America

This paper meets the requirements of
ANSI/NISO Z39.48-1992 (Permanence of Paper).

To Chris, who bared a part of herself that she normally keeps hidden in order to help me get a handle on these characters. You have more strength and heart than I can express with words.

CHAPTER 1

"ROSIE, YOU need to hurry or you're going to miss the bus." Newton DeSantis checked his watch for what felt like the millionth time in the last minute.

"I'm coming, Daddy," Rose called back, coming down the stairs. She had insisted on dressing herself, and Newton thought his eyes were going to bleed out all over the floor. Pink, orange, neon purple—all on his kid at the same time. "I dressed like a unicorn," she said as she reached the bottom, then turned around as though she were a ballerina on stage.

Newton wiped his brow of the sweat that threatened, but then shrugged the worry away. So what? If she wanted to wear that outfit, he wasn't going to fight her. Newton was smart enough to pick his battles with his seven-year-old daughter, and this wasn't one of them.

"Eric," he called.

His son came in from the family room with a soft grumble, where he had undoubtedly been playing video games. He had his backpack, was dressed, and even looked ready. "Are you ready to go, Rosie?" Eric asked as he came over to take her hand. She pulled her hand back. Rosie wanted to be a big girl and was at the "I want to do everything myself" stage. Eric, at nine, just wanted to get where he wanted to go.

"Remember the rules, Rosie," Newton admonished lightly. Both of them had said they were big enough to walk themselves to the bus stop. Apparently some of the kids at school had been giving Rosie a little grief and calling her a baby or some such crap. "You need to stay with Eric until you get on the bus." Not that he wasn't going to be watching, but neither of the kids needed to know that.

"Yes, Daddy," she said with an epic roll of her eyes.

He got a hug from each of them, and then Rosie and Eric left the house and walked just down the street. They would get on the bus in front of Mrs. Tanner's house, and Newton knew she would be watching as well. She always made sure the kids were safe. It was probably a habit from when her kids were little. Newton watched from the front door and waited for the bus to come down the street. His kids got on, and he turned away. He closed and locked the front door before taking his bag and heading through the house toward the back, using his cane to take some of the weight off his aching left foot.

Newton got into his car in the garage, putting his things inside, and backed out, grateful for the new door opener he'd gotten himself for his last birthday. With the door closed, he continued on to work.

Today was a courthouse day, and he was never a huge fan of those. Newton had given testimony on many occasions, and that never bothered him too much—it was familiar territory. What he didn't like was the uncertain outcomes. As a social worker, he spent his days mostly with women who were trying to get themselves, and often their children, out of bad home situations. The case today should be fairly cut and dried, but with hearings, attorneys, and judges, he had learned he could never truly predict an outcome.

The unpredictability was what he hated. Newton had come to rely on order, routines, and as much normalcy as he could get in his life. As few surprises as he could muster was an incredible pleasure. Still, he loved his job and the fact that he was helping people. It was what he had been driven to do for the last nearly eighteen years.

He parked in the courthouse lot, took a deep breath, and slowly got out of the car, bringing his case and his cane along with him.

Newton hated the fact that he had to use the damned cane, but it was becoming a fact of life and there was very little he could do about it. He'd asked about surgery, but he'd had plenty of those already, and now the doctors simply shook their heads, telling him there was nothing more they could do. Just another in a long line of issues he had to incorporate into his life. So that was what he did—worked with what he had and kept moving forward.

"Morning," Newton told the security officers at the courthouse door as he placed his things on the belt to be scanned. Then he walked through the scanner, which of course went off the way it did each time. Newton stepped to the side, and they wanded him before letting him get his things and move on. It was the same routine each time, and even though all of the security men knew him, he went through it because it was their job. In a way, the routine made him feel safer inside the building, even though deep down he knew it was a false safety. If someone were determined…. He pushed that thought from his mind and headed for the elevator to the second floor.

TWO HOURS later, Newton sat on a hard seat in the back and tried not to squirm and drop his cane from his lap, even though his leg kept falling asleep. The lawyers were arguing the merits of their cases, and since Newton had already testified, he got to sit in the courtroom. He kept his hands in his lap, but his fingers were restless, since he channeled all his nervous energy into them.

The client involved in this hearing wasn't one of Newton's, but because of the circumstances, he had been asked to testify, and now he was invested in the outcome. By rights, he should have left and let the justice system do its thing, but he couldn't.

Okay, if he was honest with himself, part of the reason for him staying was the case and another part was because he got to watch Chase Matthews in action. Chase was an attorney, and in this case, he had been assigned by the judge to represent a client of Newton's colleague Jill. The man was eloquent and passionate, and when he turned to where Newton could view him, Newton swore he could see his intense blue-gray eyes from across the room. The man had presence and was a legal force of nature. He didn't just talk—he used his entire body, his whole being, putting everything he had into each sentence, each argument, and did it with the sheer magnetism of his presence. It was enticing and enthralling to watch, like an actor giving the performance of their life as Hamlet, or a figure skater presenting a program in the Olympic final that left the viewers breathless.

Newton checked his watch and sighed. As much as he wanted to stay, he needed to get back to work. Sitting around watching Chase do his job was not the best use of his time. He quietly got up, walked to the door, pulled it open, and stepped outside. He made sure it closed silently and then went down the hall, where he placed his things on a bench. He took his phone out of the bottom of his bag and turned it on. There were four voicemails, and he skimmed through the speech-to-text so he could return the call that was most important.

"Angela, what's going on?" he asked as soon as she answered. He could almost feel her panic coming through the phone. Gasps reached his ears, following by heaves of breath.

"His parents—" She gulped, then gasped some more.

"It's okay. Just take a minute and breathe. Whatever it is, we'll be all right. I promise you." Newton sat down, his patience coming forward. "Are you okay? Do I need to get you some help?"

"Yes. But I'm okay. I can talk now." She was still seconds from breathlessness. "I'm sorry to bother you." She now sobbed into the phone, and Newton wished he was there with her to try to comfort in person. But that wasn't possible at the moment.

"Are you home alone?" Newton tried to think who he could get to be with her. Angela was a new client, and much of her world had been pulled out from under her a year ago. Her case had been reassigned to him a month ago because the previous caseworker had been useless and was let go.

"Yes. I'll be okay." She seemed stronger now.

"Put down the phone, go get yourself a tissue, and have a drink of water. Don't forget to breathe, and then you pick up the phone again and tell me what happened." He kept his own worry out of his voice. Angela needed him to be strong and calm and to keep the darkness that lingered around the edges of his consciousness like constantly moving tendrils at bay. Most of the time he was very good at that, but strong emotion seemed to give them force, and they'd try to grow and work their way forward. He could already feel his jitteriness increasing, but he looked around the marble-lined hall, with its imposing size and decoration, drawing strength from the solidity of the building.

She stepped away, and when she returned, she spoke more clearly. "Reggie's parents have decided that they're going to fight me for custody of Marcie and Debbie." She sniffed but remained in control. "They're going to try to prove I'm unfit."

Newton had heard this tactic before. "First, that's very difficult to do and isn't going to happen." Angela had issues with alcohol as well as mental health, all of which she was getting help for. She was eight months sober and had her AA chip to prove it. She carried it with her everywhere she went. And she had been taking her meds for years.

"They told me they are also going to enter the divorce as Reggie's advocates. They feel that their son's rights need to be protected and that he should be able to see his children." The quivering in her voice was back.

"Okay. First thing, grandparents have no parental rights in this state. And second, do they understand that Reggie isn't interested in those girls? He admits he never wanted to be a parent. Are they completely stupid?" He shouldn't have asked the last question, but it slipped out. "They do realize that he actually said that in court? What do they expect, that they're going to force him to see the girls?" Reggie had left when the strain of the kids became more than he could stand.

"I don't know. But I need to get a lawyer, and I can't afford one. There's barely enough money to keep the girls and me fed and a roof over our heads." She sniffed. "I actually thought about walking to the store around the corner as soon as the girls left for school. I called my sponsor instead, but...." The tears were so close once again, and Newton wanted to try to help her feel better.

"They can't do anything right away. You stay calm and go to a meeting. Get yourself surrounded by supporters. As for a lawyer, I'll check at the office and see what resources I can call on." He wasn't sure what he could do, but Newton would try. Angela and her family had already been through hell for the last year after being abandoned, and they didn't deserve more. "I need to go because court is letting out and I need to be quiet, but I'll call you back as soon as I can." He hung up after she agreed. Newton dropped his phone in his bag and would have gotten up to hobble to the exit, but his foot ached, so he turned to elevate it on the bench for a few minutes and closed his eyes. He just needed some time for the blood to start flowing normally again.

The door to the courtroom opened, and Chase Matthews strode out, looking amazing in a suit that probably cost as much as Newton made in a month. The man had style and knew how to dress, which made him look damn fine, that was for sure.

Newton scrambled off the bench and hobble-ran up to him. "Mr. Matthews."

Chase stopped, turning around, his electric gaze falling onto Newton, sending a thrill running up his spine. "Can I help you?" he asked in a voice that could melt butter.

"Not me, but one of my clients," Newton said as he used the cane for balance. "She needs a lawyer, and…."

Chase shook his head. "Oh no. I've done my pro bono work for the year, and I have real clients that I need to get to work on." The eyes that Newton had thought so intense and expressive grew cold, and he suppressed a shiver. "I only took this case because I was required to by Judge Harker." He turned to walk away, but Newton was pissed off enough that he grabbed his arm. "Now see here—"

"Look. I have a mother with two kids who need help, desperately. She's trying to keep her children. Her husband, soon to be ex, is in prison for abusing those adorable girls, and now she's got to fight his parents because they feel their son's rights aren't being represented." Newton didn't let go, and he did his best to ignore the woodsy cologne that wafted around him.

"I've done my part. I have a practice that I need to return to and clients who are paying me to represent them. I can't just take on another case like that right now. I'm sorry, but I've done what I can." Chase shrugged off Newton's hand, strode toward the elevator, and pressed the call button. Newton got his bag and made his way over to join Chase as he waited. "God, this is slow."

"Yes, I know. That gives me plenty of time to try to convince you to change your mind." Newton flashed a little smile.

"You don't take no for an answer, do you?" Chase asked, turning back to watch the doors, probably willing them to slide open so he could get away.

"If I did, I wouldn't be able to help my clients. And these people need help. Angela's in-laws have money, and they are willing to use it to get their way and do what isn't in the interest of these girls. They were five and seven when their father hurt them." Newton was laying it on thick, but in his job, often all he had was the human angle, and he was very good at tugging at people's heartstrings.

The elevator doors slid open, and they stepped inside. Chase pushed the button to go down, and the doors slid closed. Newton knew he had just a few seconds to make his case before Chase made his escape. "You know justice isn't fair, as much as we hope it can be…."

"Life isn't fair," Chase said, then sighed. "I can't take on any more work right now. My caseload is full and I'm working twelve-hour days as it is." He shifted his weight.

"And you're not the only one." Newton looked down at his old suit and partially rumpled shirt because he hadn't had enough time to iron it that morning, with breakfast to make, getting the kids off to school… everything.

"I'm sorry." Chase stepped off the elevator and was about to walk away.

Newton was desperate. "When was the last time you had a home-cooked meal?" It was a Hail Mary shot, but he had to go for it. Guys like Chase ate out or at their desk, and the food they consumed could be pretty crappy. Newton would know, because he did the same thing when he was at work.

Chase stopped and turned around.

"Come over to the house, meet Angela, and then you can decide. I'll even cook."

Chase rubbed his temple, and Newton could tell he was trying to make a choice. "I…."

"What have you got to lose, except your taste buds?"

Chase smiled, and Newton knew he had him. He reached into his bag, got a card, and handed it to Chase, who got a card from his pocket and handed it over after writing a number on the back as well.

"I know I'm probably going to regret this," he said with a half smile.

"Maybe," Newton teased, pleased he had gotten a shot. "I'll text you my address. So, tomorrow at six?"

Chase agreed, then turned, striding hurriedly out of the courthouse.

His mother had been right: "If you feed them, they will come."

Granted, he wasn't totally convinced that Chase wouldn't blow him off with some excuse that sounded really urgent, but he had gotten his foot in the door, and that was probably all he could expect.

Newton left the courthouse, heading to his car. Once he was inside, he texted Chase his address, the time, and asked if he was allergic to anything. Then he made a call to Angela.

"I think I might have found you a lawyer."

"A good one?" she asked.

"If he'll take the case, one of the best. I've lured him to my house with the promise of food, but I'm not a really good cook. I've spent the last decade either making bottles or cooking for the kids and eating what they have." Newton felt a little bad about misrepresenting himself, but he could get high-end takeout and serve it on his own plates if he had to. "You and the girls come to dinner tomorrow. I want him to see your family and see it's worth his while to help you." It was harder to turn someone down face-to-face. "He'll be here at six, so come a little early. This is a full-court family-and-kids press."

Angela laughed. It was still tense, but with a hint of happiness around the edges. "You'll sure go to lengths to get what you want."

"I try." Newton ended the call and started his car, going to his office to try to get a full day's work done in an afternoon.

"DAD, WILL there be kids?" Eric asked as he set the table.

Newton rolled his eyes. "Yes. I already told you." He put his hand on his son's shoulder. "You need to listen to me. You get involved in the television or in your games, and you don't pay attention to anything around you." He pulled out a chair and sat down, grateful to be off his feet. "You're getting older, and you need to listen. You'll be a lot happier if you pay more attention to what's happening around you." He made sure that Eric was watching him and that he had his full attention. "There are two girls coming. They're six and eight, but they have been through some bad things. We don't ask about them, and you need to not yell or run around." That was like asking the tide to stop rising, but he had to try.

"Do they play dolls?" Rosie asked. Newton smiled and nodded. "Then I'll get some of mine that they can play with while they're here." She ran away toward the stairs and then came back. "I'll share, but they can't keep them. They're my dollies," she pronounced and raced toward the other room.

Newton chuckled under his breath. That was both happy and sad at the same time. "Of course not. Those are your toys, and it's really nice of you to share."

Rosie had been in a foster home, and because of her vision issues, which were largely corrected by glasses and regular visits to the eye doctor, she hadn't been adopted. Newton had taken one look at the special little girl with the Coke-bottle glasses perched on her little nose and the band around her head to hold them in place and had fallen in love instantly. Dozens of appointments and a number of prescription changes had corrected some of her vision issues, but the trauma of the foster homes lingered, including the fact that her toys had often been appropriated or simply hadn't been hers and hadn't moved with her.

"Okay, Dad. I'll try," Eric said.

Newton's brain shifted back to their conversation. "Okay." He hugged him. "Go ahead and finish setting the table, and then you need to help me with dinner." Newton needed all the help he could get. He'd pulled out a number of recipes and decided to try one for something called Hawaiian chicken. It was currently in the oven, and the scent was even more enticing than he had hoped it would be.

"Okay," Eric said and got back to work.

Rosie joined him in the kitchen a few minutes later, and Newton gave each of them a task. They were easy, but making dinner, even something as simple as chicken nuggets and salad, was usually done together.

Newton checked his phone, expecting a cancellation from Chase at any time, but it stayed quiet. He was almost finished getting things ready when the doorbell rang. Newton let Angela and the girls in the house. He introduced the kids, and Rosie took the girls up to her room to play.

"I brought some dessert." Angela followed him into the kitchen and set a cake carrier on the counter. She lifted the lid, and the scent of rich chocolate had his stomach rumbling. "I figured I'd pull out all the stops."

"Awesome." Newton was a little nervous and checked his dish again, thinking he'd give it ten more minutes and then it would be ready to come out, just about the time Chase should arrive. Newton closed the oven and went to finish the salad Eric had abandoned to go back to his video games. "I suspect he's going to ask you about your case. Be truthful and don't be afraid to lay it on thick. He needs to know what Reggie did and what you're up against."

She pursed her lips and nodded. "I know I'm going to have to tell this story a lot, but it's not easy. It sucks knowing their father could just walk away from them."

"It's going to be even harder in court." The doorbell rang, and Newton girded his loins, as it were, and went to answer it. The girls came down the stairs, probably to see who was there.

Chase stood on his steps in sharply pressed tan slacks and a dark blue sweater smoothed over his torso. He looked like something straight out of a magazine.

"Thank you for coming," Newton said when he remembered he was supposed to be talking and not just staring. He motioned, and Chase stepped inside. Newton had made sure the kids had picked up their toys and that the house was relatively clean, but it was difficult to sweep away the effects of two young kids completely. "This is Angela Wilson," Newton said by way of introduction. "And her daughters. Marcie, and this is Debbie." He smiled at her youngest, but she tried to hide behind her mother.

"Chase Matthews. It's good to meet you." They shook hands as Newton closed the door. "Dang, it smells good in here. I love pineapple... and chocolate." He knelt down to say hello to both of Angela's girls, but they stayed close to their mother, their eyes as wide as saucers.

"Why don't you have a seat? I can bring you something to drink and then finish up dinner." Newton peeked into the family room. "Eric, I need your help." This time Eric turned off the television and followed him into the kitchen. "Find out what our guests would like to drink while I get dinner out."

Eric hurried away, and Newton got the Pyrex dish out of the oven and set it on the burners. The sauce bubbled nicely, and the topping was golden brown, just like the recipe said it should be. He took off his oven mitts, closed the door, and together with Eric, got waters for his guests and brought the glasses into the living room.

"Girls, it's about dinnertime," he called into the other room, and the three of them trooped in. Newton and Angela ushered them into the dining room and to places at the table. Angela sat between her daughters, and Newton did the same with his kids on the other side of the table, with Chase at the end. Since the casserole was superhot, he dished up for Chase and then handed the spoon to Angela.

"Daddy, what do we call him?" Rosie stage-whispered, pointing to Chase.

"How about Mr. Chase, and you can call her Ms. Angela, okay?" Newton looked at the others. Angela nodded, and Chase seemed surprised, but nodded as well.

Rosie seemed satisfied and took a bite of the chicken. "Mr. Chase, are you a teacher? You dress like Mr. Baxter." She smiled.

"No. I'm a lawyer."

Rosie frowned. "That's too bad."

"Honey." Newton had no idea what was going on. "That wasn't nice."

Rosie leaned close, near tears. "But we're supposed to kill all the lawyers. That's what they said on television." She puffed out her lower lip, and Newton turned to Eric.

"What were you watching that you weren't supposed to?" Newton demanded, and Eric had the grace to look sheepish. "If it was *Law and Order*, I'm…." He swallowed the threat because Eric got the message. "Honey, that was a show for grown-ups, and it was meant as a joke." *Oh good Lord.*

"Oh." Rosie went back to eating like there was nothing wrong.

Chase turned away from the table, trying not to laugh but failing. The sound was like the ringing of a large bell: deep, resonant, clear, and a joy to listen to. Rosie seemed completely happy now, and Newton and Angela shared a look of understanding.

"You never know what these kids will say," Angela said, then bit her lower lip. Newton knew what she was thinking, but that conversation was for when there weren't little ears around. Her daughters ate but didn't say much. Newton wondered if it was because Chase was a stranger. Not that he could blame them.

Angela's youngest, Debbie, whispered something to her, and Angela nodded. "Why don't you ask Rosie if she's done, and then you can all go play."

Rosie slipped off her chair, and the three girls went upstairs to Rosie's room. Eric was still eating—that boy was developing a hollow leg, which Newton was pleased to see. He cleaned his plate and then asked to be excused.

"Of course, but keep the volume down." He knew his son well.

"This was wonderful," Chase said as he took a break from eating. "I haven't had anything home-cooked in a while." He smiled and turned to Angela. "I think we should talk about your case. That is why I'm here."

She nodded but seemed to pale.

"This is hard for her still," Newton said.

"Yes, I know. But I need the facts in the case, and it's unfortunate, but the justice system has little concern for feelings or how much people are hurting. Take your time."

Angela glanced toward the stairs. "My husband, hopefully ex-husband soon, he just left us. Reggie...." She used her napkin to wipe her eyes. "My youngest, Debbie, told me that he would leave them alone when I wasn't there. While he was away, the house caught fire because he left something on the stove."

"He's legally neglectful, tried and convicted," Newton added quietly.

"I filed for divorce because I need to separate my life from his, and the girls deserve a chance at some distance and to be able to recover. Reggie said he wouldn't contest it. But then his parents decided to throw their money around, and now they are trying to say that I'm an unfit mother, that I'm trying to cut away their son's rights and their rights.... He neglected his daughters and left us to try to save his own skin—how can he have rights?" She sipped some water. "I only want my daughters to have a chance at some happiness."

Newton stepped in for Angela's sake. "We have Angela and her daughters in therapy, and the girls are progressing. I know they've been quiet because you're a new person, but...." As if on cue, laughter drifted down from upstairs, all three girls giggling and squealing in delight. It was a gorgeous sound. "You can hear that things are improving."

"I'm doing my best to keep all of this from them. They don't need this ugliness. But my in-laws are making it hard." Angela set down her napkin. "They actually told me that they wanted the girls to spend the weekend with them, and that while they were there, they could take them to visit their daddy." She blinked, her expression growing fierce. "Like hell they will. Those idiots want to take my girls to visit someone who almost got them killed. Over my dead body." She shook with justified rage.

Chase sat quietly, listening. "Family law in Wisconsin isn't as convoluted as most states. Thank goodness. Since he's been convicted of neglecting the girls, we can petition to sever his parental rights. As for the grandparents, we can allow them visits, but with conditions and, if necessary, under supervision. We can also petition the courts for a ruling that the girls are not to see their father until they are old enough to decide on their own if they want to."

Angela half smiled. "Is it that easy?"

"Things are never that easy, but we can make a good case." Chase drank some water himself and seemed to be thinking. "Grandparents have no particular rights here. This happens quite often. Grandparents step in, thinking they have some special legal dispensation, but they don't."

All three girls traipsed in carrying dolls and sat at their places. "Can we have cake, Daddy?" Rosie asked.

"It's chocolate," Debbie offered, her first words to the adults since arriving.

"Do you like chocolate?" Chase asked her.

She nodded, clutching one of Rosie's dolls to her. "I like it this much." Her arms went out for a few seconds and then she clutched the doll again.

"I like it that much too." Chase winked at her, and she smiled a real smile. "How about you?" he asked Marcie, who nodded.

Angela sighed, putting her arms around both of them. "They used to be such happy girls, but then they changed. Now they're quiet and shy." She hugged each of them. "It's okay. Mr. Chase is a nice man, I promise you."

Both girls nodded but didn't say much more to Chase. It seemed he'd gotten what he was going to get out of them. Newton had met them more than once, and he hadn't gotten either of them to talk much more than tonight either.

"I'll cut the cake," Newton offered, and went into the kitchen. He brought plates to the table and then the cake, setting it in the center. The scent must have drawn Eric, because he came and sat in his place. Newton cut small pieces for the girls and Eric, then ones for Chase, Angela, and himself. He got forks and refilled glasses before sitting back down.

"This is awesome," Chase said as he ate.

"Angela baked it. She's amazing with things like that." Newton hadn't known her that long, but if she could make this amazing cake, one where neither of his kids said a word while wolfing it down, she knew her stuff.

"Is it good?" Chase asked Debbie, who smiled and nodded, her lips covered with chocolate.

"Mama bakes real good," Marcie said, and she took another bite. At least both girls had said something and seemed to be relaxing a little.

Newton slowly ate his cake, watching that Eric didn't gulp his and that Rosie didn't make a huge mess. "Are you all done?" Newton asked the girls. "Then go wash up and you can play." He cut Eric another small piece of cake because he didn't seem to be able to get enough to eat. Eric took his plate and left the table to play video games, leaving the adults alone once again.

"Do you think you can help?" Newton asked Chase. He could see the indecision in his eyes.

"Yes," he finally answered, sharing a smile with Angela before turning his intense gaze on Newton. "You sure don't take no for an answer when you really want something." He didn't seem angry or upset. Chase passed Angela a business card. "Call my office and make an appointment for next week. Bring all the documentation. We'll develop a strategy and counter these arguments before they can really take hold." Chase pushed away from the table. "I need to get going." He stood, with Newton and Angela both doing the same.

Newton saw Chase to the door. "Thank you for helping her," he said softly. "I know I came on strong, but...."

Chase actually smiled. "You're a man who follows his passions, I can see that. You have strong beliefs and are willing to fight for them. That's something worth admiring, and—"

Angela hurried over. "There's something wrong with Eric. He's having trouble breathing."

Newton hurried to the family room, where Eric sat in the chair, gasping for breath. Newton took his pulse and found it racing.

"What do you need me to do?" Angela asked.

"I need to get Eric to Children's Hospital right away," Newton said with remarkable calmness.

"Should I call an ambulance?" Chase asked.

"No. They aren't going to know what to do for him," Newton said as Chase lifted Eric into his arms and carried him through the house. "Rosie," he called, "go get in the car, right now! We have to take care of Eric."

"I'll get him into the car," Chase said.

"We have to go. Rosie, hurry, we need to go." His heart raced as Chase carried Eric to the car, thinking only of his son. This had happened before, but it had been months since he'd had an attack. They used to scare the hell out of him, but he knew what to do now. So did Rosie, who brought the backpack he kept in Eric's closet and climbed into her car seat. Newton got Eric settled in the back and told him to stay calm. Angela was already leaving the house with the girls as Newton climbed in the car. Chase raced back and locked the house.

Newton jumped when the passenger door opened and Chase got in, buckling up. "Let's get going."

"You don't need to…." Newton began even as his hand put the car into reverse and he backed out of the drive, then took off down the road like a bat out of hell.

"Can you talk to me, Eric?" Newton asked.

"Yes," he said raspily.

"What do you need me to do?" Chase asked, turning toward the back seat.

Newton didn't take his eyes off the road. Time was of the essence. "He needs to stay alert if possible. Eric, we're only ten minutes from the hospital. Just concentrate on breathing as best you can."

Eric started coughing—wet, painful coughs that Newton felt right along with him. He knew his lungs were filling with fluid and he had to get him to the hospital.

"Eric, buddy, are you still with me?" Chase reached back. "Just nod for me. Great. Keep your eyes open if you can and take my hand." Chase held Eric's hand, and as soon as they reached the freeway, Newton floored it. Traffic was light, and he knew this route well, pulling off five miles down, exiting, and making the turn into the hospital downtown and right into Emergency.

Newton ran around, lifted Eric out of the back, and carried him inside. He and Rosie had done this enough that he knew she would be right behind him with the backpack.

"I take it you've done this before?" Chase said.

Newton nodded as he helped Eric up to the desk. He gave his name and Eric's, and was escorted right into the back. Thank God Jerry Young was on duty. He had helped Eric before, and while the nurse got the admission information, Jerry was already issuing instructions for an IV with saline. He put it in and got it going.

Newton sat next to the bed while the nurses hooked Eric up to the monitors. Usually the first thing that they would do under the circumstances was administer oxygen, but that wasn't going to help Eric. His lungs were flooded, and getting him saline and regulating his internal fluids emptied his lungs. Oxygen alone wasn't going to do anything for him.

Newton stressed as he watched Eric's once-elevated heart rate, now very low, start to come up again, and as the minutes passed, his breathing improved. Only then did he look around and realize that Rosie wasn't with him.

"Where is Rosie?" Newton asked Macy, one of the nurses he'd come to know. Hell, by now he knew most of the ER staff.

She leaned closer. "She's out in the waiting room sitting next to a gorgeous man with the most intense eyes I have ever seen. Are you dating him? Because if you're not, I'd like a shot at his fineness." She winked.

"He's a lawyer, and no, I'm not dating him." Newton never dated anyone. Between the kids and his own issues, they didn't stick around for very long. "He was meeting with one of my clients at the house when Eric had his episode, and he came along."

"Do you want me to bring them back?"

"Would you?" Newton didn't want to leave Eric.

Macy nodded, leaving the room. She returned a few minutes later with Rosie and Chase behind her. Rosie certainly seemed to have opened up to Chase, rattling on about God knows what, with Chase listening to every word.

"Hey, buddy, are you going to be okay?" Chase asked, coming to stand near where Newton sat. Rosie set the backpack beside his chair and climbed onto Newton's lap, settling in as though she had had enough excitement.

"Yes," Eric answered. "Needles suck, though."

Chase leaned closer and stage-whispered, "I don't like them either, so you're pretty brave." He patted Eric's shoulder and got a smile in return.

"Do you need me to arrange a ride home for you?" Newton asked Chase. When he'd come to dinner, Chase most certainly hadn't been expecting this kind of action.

"I'm fine." Chase smiled at Eric, who closed his eyes. The monitors told Newton that he was just sleeping and not losing consciousness, so he let him rest. These episodes took a great deal out of him.

"Do you want to see if we can find a cafeteria where we can get something to drink?" Chase asked Rosie, who perked right up and took Chase's hand. For a second, a jab of jealousy stabbed at Newton, but it died quickly, even though he wondered what it would be like to feel that hand in his. "We'll be back in a few minutes," Chase said as he and Rosie left the ER area.

"Are you feeling any better?" Newton asked quietly when Eric opened his eyes.

"Yes." It was apparent that Eric was breathing much better, and his color was improving.

Newton sat back, his heart rate returning to normal as the danger to Eric passed. The IV drip continued, and Newton tried not to stare at it. But with Eric now dozing and the room quiet, he had little to look at.

"Daddy," Rosie said as she came in the room, followed by Chase, who handed him a cup. "We brought this for you."

"Thank you," Newton said to Chase and sipped from the cup. "He should be all right now." Rosie climbed onto his lap.

"How often does this happen?" Chase asked.

"The last time was six months ago." Newton smoothed the hair away from Eric's forehead. He needed to get him a haircut. "He has POTS—postural orthostatic tachycardia syndrome—and is one of the youngest people ever diagnosed with it." Newton took Eric's hand. "It's been two years since diagnosis, but we've been dealing with it for longer. They tell us that it might be getting worse right now because of the prepuberty hormones and things. But they're guessing, since most of the people who have this syndrome are women." He was dreading Eric's teenage years because of the sheer unpredictability. Newton set his cup on the stand next to the bed and held Rosie's and Eric's hands.

"Isn't that a disease where people get dizzy when they stand?" Chase asked.

"No. It's a syndrome with a collection of symptoms that can vary. Eric has it worse than most, who just get dizzy when they stand. The doctors have been reluctant to put him on medication because they don't know what it will do to someone so young. We've been holding off as much as we can. He was having them every three months or so—this was six, so it's working in our favor, at least for now." This was so much for a young kid to go through.

Rosie curled against his chest, and the room grew quiet. Newton wasn't up to talking, and once the IV was finished, they discussed running a second, but it seemed it wasn't necessary. Eric was stable, and giving him too many fluids only brought him additional issues later.

"We're going to let him rest and keep him for a little while longer before we let him go," Jerry explained, and even coaxed a smile from Eric when he promised he'd remove the needle soon.

THERE WAS another hour at the hospital and then the drive home to get through. Newton had both kids in bed, with Eric's upper body propped up slightly on pillows. He watched him for a few seconds and then left the room. It was going to be a night of little sleep as he got up every hour or so just to make sure Eric was okay. Half closing the door so he could hear if Eric was in distress, he returned downstairs to where Chase waited on the sofa.

"I know this was more than you bargained for." He didn't sit down, because he wasn't likely to get back up. "Would you like something to drink? I have a bottle of juice, water, a few diet sodas I hid from the kids...."

"Soda would be great. That's all I usually like to drink when I'm driving."

Chase had a point. Newton grabbed both sodas out of the back of the drawer in the refrigerator, took them to the living room, and handed one to Chase. Then he sat down with a sigh. "I appreciate you going tonight. Rosie really likes you."

"She's pretty special," Chase said. "Both of your kids are." He opened the can and sipped.

"Yeah. They're the center of my life." Newton closed his eyes. So much for so long had been near chaos. "Eric crossed my path when he was in foster care—they both did. Eric had breathing issues as a baby, and his allergy profile is off the charts. You won't find nuts of any kind anywhere in this house, or coconut—none of that. When I first got him, he wheezed and coughed a lot. But with the help of doctors, we eliminated a lot of his allergens from the house, including the fact that the home where he was living had a cat and he's allergic to those too." He drank some of the soda and set the can on the table. "No one wanted to adopt him and take on all the issues he had."

Chase smiled to his incredible eyes. "And you took one look at him and that was the end of it."

"Pretty much. I knew he was going to be a challenge, but we eliminated the allergens from the environment and his diet, made sure we limited sweets and spicy food, and added sodium because it helps regulate and retain fluids and actually helps prevent attacks. At least we think so." Newton sighed. "And Rosie... she wound me around her little finger with ease."

"So neither of them is biologically yours?" Chase asked.

"No. I haven't had a partner in…." He rolled his eyes. "A very long time. I have my work, and since I adopted the kids, they have my energy." They gave love without expecting something else in return. Newton was under no illusions; he knew what his life was, and he had his feet planted firmly on the ground. There was the work he loved, and Rosie with her needs, and Eric with his. The love those two children gave him was more than he ever thought possible. "Rosie's adoption was finalized a year ago. Do you have kids?"

Chase shook his head. "I guess I'm too busy. I want to be a partner in my firm, so I work way too much and I'm too danged career-focused. I had a boyfriend in college, but that crashed and burned in spectacular fashion. Since then…." He shrugged, and Newton nodded. He understood. "Sometimes it's just easier to work on other things. Like anyone is really going to want to see me after eight o'clock at night and then have me up at six and out the door by seven."

He's gay. For some reason a flutter raced through Newton and sent his belly into little butterfly wings of excitement. Of course it didn't mean anything, and he had enough in his life at the moment without getting involved with anyone. He'd told himself many times that his life was full enough. But lately those reassurances hadn't rung as true as they once had, especially when the kids had been younger. "Yeah, well, there are no off hours with being a parent." The room grew still, and he listened for any sound from upstairs, but all remained quiet.

"Well, maybe you could take a little time off to go to dinner?" Chase asked.

Newton stilled, wondering if he'd heard properly. "You're asking me out?" he asked, almost pulling on his ears to make sure they were working properly.

"Why not? You must need a little time for yourself every once in a while, and I sure as hell could use a chance to go out with someone who isn't a colleague or a client." Chase finished his soda.

"Sure. We can try to do that." Newton could attempt to find someone to watch the kids for a few hours. Newton tried to think of the last time he had been out with anyone for any reason. "But I don't get it. Why you'd want to go out with me?" He had plenty of baggage, more than just two amazing kids.

Chase chuckled as he walked to the door. "You're tenacious, Newton. I haven't met anyone in a long time who would take me on the way you did at the courthouse the other day. I told you no, and you didn't give up and pled your case anyway." Chase pulled open the door. "I'll call you tomorrow, and we can set up an evening for dinner." He paused. "And just so you know, don't expect me to cook like you did tonight. Not unless you want to end up in the hospital for a very different reason. My cooking is lethal." Chase said goodbye and left the house, closing the door behind him.

Newton locked it and made sure Chase was gone before turning off the outside lights and then heading up to bed. He was inordinately pleased that he was going to be seeing Chase again, and it put a smile on his lips that lasted until he fell to sleep.

CHAPTER 2

CHASE SAT at the polished desk in his office and hung up the phone yet again. He had made dozens of calls that morning, and he was waiting for the return of a final one. The stack of documents for him to review kept getting taller, and he made inroads as he waited, marking some for his associates and paralegals to handle.

"Why are you so danged happy?" his assistant, William, asked after knocking and then coming in. "It's been one hell of a day. The partners are all meeting as though there is some crisis brewing."

There was, but it had nothing to do with Chase, thank God. One of the firm's high-profile corporate suits had hit a major snag, and that meant that the huge payoff they had been anticipating probably wasn't going to materialize. Not that Chase would see any of that anyway, because he wasn't a partner. But he'd predicted exactly what would happen, and when he'd taken it to Milton Howard, the senior partner, Milton had listened to him and gone ahead anyway.

"They have their problems, and we have ours." Chase turned his attention to the paperwork once again, handing an organized file to William. "This is for Anne. My notes are inside—the same for these for Denton. Tell them both to go ahead and get the paperwork ready to file. I want these wrapped up this week."

"Is there anything else?" William asked as he held the files. "Like why you're smiling?" He turned and closed the door. "Okay. You've been grinning like you just won the lotto and don't need this pressure cooker any longer. What gives?" He leaned over the desk. "Did you find another place to work? Will you take me with you?" William was sometimes overly dramatic, but only with Chase, and it could put a smile on his face even on the toughest days.

"No. I'm not leaving, but if I were, I would definitely take you with me," Chase said. There was no way he could do this job without William's efficiency or his daily dose of sunshine. "Now, stop digging for information and get back to work." He raised his eyebrows, and William just smiled.

"I can take a hint." William pulled open the door.

"About as well as I can dance ballet," Chase retorted.

William nearly dropped the file folders. Chase was a notoriously bad dancer. At the firm Christmas party last year, Gwen Howard, the wife of the senior partner, had insisted he dance with her. It lasted about two minutes and ended with her hobbling off the dance floor and Milton telling her that he'd warned her.

"Good one," William said through his chuckles. "I hear Milton's wife is able to walk normally now." He closed the door behind him before Chase could throw something at him.

Chase answered his ringing phone and got back to work, but even the call from a ridiculous attorney, who had no case but was still trying to wheedle some sort of deal, wasn't going to put him off his day.

He worked quietly for another hour until the call he was waiting for was returned. He sighed and smiled because he loved it when things came together this easily. Chase messaged Newton about dinner just to make sure that they were still on. He received an immediate answer that the sitter had confirmed, and Newton asked if he wanted to meet at the restaurant. Chase answered that he'd pick Newton up at six, then made another call, this one almost equally good news.

"Angela, it's Chase Matthews," he said. "I was able to speak with the attorney for your in-laws, and it seems they've had a change of heart." He smiled.

"Really?" she asked. "That doesn't sound like them."

No. It probably didn't. "They changed their tune once they saw all my requests for discovery about their finances, tax returns, investments, and medical histories. After all, they raised a convicted abuser. What if there's something in the family medical or mental health history that led to that? I also asked for school records of both of them, and I told them we would be talking to friends and colleagues to determine the kind of parents they were. They raised a thoughtless, selfish ass once—what if they do it again?" He was already smirking. "It seems they weren't as keen to have someone looking into their past and all the things they might have done." Chase was just getting started. "I also informed him that if they should lose, and that was highly likely, it was also almost a certainty that they would never see their granddaughters again."

Angela swallowed. "I would never do that."

"I know, but they don't. Anyway, his parents have decided they are no longer going to be a party to the divorce, and it seems the other matters are going to be dropped as well." Chase knew how to handle people like them—bury them in requests and threaten equally invasive counter motions. "They thought that this would be easy and that they could scare you into getting what they wanted. When that didn't work, they folded like a house of cards. My suggestion is to do nothing until they call you. And then say that they can visit their granddaughters, but only with supervision and under controlled circumstances. Be nice but firm, and we'll see what their next move is, if any." He was pretty pleased up to this point.

"Oh God, that's…." She heaved a huge sigh through the line. "I can't tell you what a relief it is. They used to be nice, but as soon as Reggie was arrested and then convicted, everything was my fault. I wasn't a good enough wife and I didn't look after him…. It was like he was the abuser, but I was the one at fault for it."

"I see that all the time." And he had experienced it firsthand. Chase had a pretty good idea what those kids were going through. It had been part of why he'd taken the case in the first place, even though he wasn't going to tell anyone that. There was no way he would let his adversaries have anything on him that they thought they could use. He had to remain strong, even when people told him stories that came way too close to home. "His parents are afraid of how his conviction will make them look, and if someone else is at fault, then Reggie can still be their little baby." Chase understood the psychology and had been able to use it against them, by threatening exactly what they had been afraid of. It was part of being a good attorney.

"I have to get the girls from the bus, but thank you so much for all your help." Angela sniffed, and Chase knew he'd done a good thing by helping her. It hadn't taken nearly as much time as he'd expected, at least so far… and he had really helped someone.

"I will still file for an order to prevent the girls from being taken to visit their father until they are of age to make that decision for themselves. That will give you legal backing to tell them that they can't try to take them to the prison, and it will help reinforce the fact that you're in charge, not them."

"Good." He could almost hear the worry slipping from her voice. "Thank you again."

"I'll be in touch when I know more." Chase ended the call and finished things up for the day.

He was getting ready to leave a little after five when Milton knocked on his door and came inside. He never went visiting, almost always calling people to his office. Chase groaned inwardly and wished he'd left five minutes earlier. It figured, the one night he had needed to get out of the office at a decent hour.

"Are you leaving?" Milton made a point of checking his watch.

"Yes. I have a dinner appointment, and I haven't left the office before seven in weeks, so I thought I'd kind of earned it." Chase wasn't going to be cowed the way most people would. He brought a great deal of revenue to the firm, and they all knew it.

"I understand you took on another pro bono case," Milton said flatly.

"Yes. It took me just a few hours. I have things well in hand, and it looks like I was able to intimidate the other side into capitulation. A few more hours to get a court order to restrict prison visitation for the abused children, and it should be over."

"That's good." Milton tapped the door frame. "Just remember that the partners will be meeting in a few months to review potential associates for partnership." The part left unsaid revolved around the fact that pro bono work wasn't going to add to his billable hours and, therefore, wasn't going to be taken into partnership consideration. "I have a new case for you... a big one."

"In family law?" Chase asked. There were high-profile divorces and things like that, but often family issues were handled quietly in the courts.

"Yes. This is a high-profile case with the potential to be explosive. Since you're on your way out, have your assistant contact Renee and book some time for tomorrow so we can discuss it." Milton leaned a little farther into the office. "This could be a case that helps define the firm, and could very well propel your career to new heights." He smiled and exited the office, leaving Chase on pins and needles. Still, he had places to be, and this new case would be waiting for him in the morning. One thing was for sure: if it was related to family law, no one else in the firm was going to touch it.

Chase packed up his things, locked his desk drawers, and left his office, putting out the trash and locking it as well.

"Leaving so early?" Hank Reynolds sneered as Chase passed his office door. The first time in weeks, and this asshole had to remark on it. "I hear the partners were talking about a big case...." The weasel was trying to insinuate that he'd lose out on it if he left. "I talked to Milton about it."

Chase chose to play dumb. "And what did he say?"

"That they were making up their minds," Hank said with a sly smile.

Chase nodded and turned to leave, then decided he couldn't leave things like that. "Then I guess I know what my meeting with him tomorrow is going to be about. Thanks, Hank." He smiled and turned away, knowing Hank was going to be fuming to no end. Chase purposely didn't look back to watch the smoke come out of his ears. Hank was a self-centered, more than a little egotistical man who tended to think the sun rose and set on his lily-white ass. Chase knew the color because he'd seen it once at the gym. *Shudder.* The guy also acted as though he were the world's best attorney, mostly because he was an ass, not because his track record was all that good.

At the elevator, Chase pressed the call button and rode down from the twentieth floor of Milwaukee's tallest building, got into his car, and drove out of the city. He was hoping to be able to drive home and change, but he'd been delayed, so he slipped off his jacket and pulled his tie off to loosen the collar of his shirt. At least he didn't look quite as buttoned-up. Before he reached Newton's home, he stopped in a parking lot, grabbed his kit from the glove compartment, and added a spritz of cologne. He also ran a comb through his hair. After checking himself in the mirror, he wondered if he should shave, but decided against it. Putting things away, he drove the rest of the way to Newton's and parked.

Chase was nervous and couldn't figure out why. They were only having dinner. It was stupid for him to get all worked up over a meal. He had them all the time and didn't sweat like a pig, but dang, it was suddenly warm, and he pulled his shirt away from his skin. Chase knocked on the door and stepped back a little. Newton opened it, and Chase gasped softly. Up until now, he'd seen Newton in casual clothes, as well as what he wore to work and court, but this…. Newton looked stunning in gray dress slacks and a plum polo shirt.

"I didn't know where we were going, so I wanted to look nice." He lowered his gaze. "Come on in. I need to get my shoes, and I'll be ready to go."

Newton moved away with his cane, and Chase wandered the room, nodding when he stepped over a pile of Legos and a doll poking out from under the sofa. He retrieved it and set it in one of the chairs, smiling as he remembered little Rosie and her grin.

"It's strange with the kids at the sitters for a few hours," Newton said when he returned. "I get so used to the level of noise they generate that I forget what real quiet is like."

"I suppose," Chase agreed softly.

"I bet your life is quiet."

Newton's comment got Chase to thinking how quiet his life was. The office bordered on dead silence. Everyone's work was intense, so talking was done in whispers. Most conversations held some level of confidentiality, so they were handled in conference rooms or behind closed doors. At home, he was alone much of the time, so the television on low was the usual level of sound, and when he brought work home, he kept it off, so there was no sound at all.

"Yeah. Sometimes too quiet," Chase half mused.

Newton chuckled. "Well, if you want noise, occasional squabbles, and drama, you're welcome to visit any time. After a few hours of them on their normal behavior, you'll go running from the room and wish you were back at home with some peace and quiet." He motioned to the door. "There are times I swear they're still and quiet only when they're in bed. Otherwise, it's a constant supply of sound."

"Is it really that bad?" Chase followed Newton outside and waited while he locked the door.

Newton smiled slyly and shook his head. "The first time Eric told me he loved me and never wanted to leave, I dang near cried...." He sighed. "And I'm man enough to admit that I did cry the first time he called me Daddy, and danged if I didn't do the same thing when Rosie did it too." Newton's voice grew deeper. "I always let the kids decide how they feel and what to call me."

"Did it take long?" Chase asked, curious. He remembered the amount of time it had taken him to relate to anyone after.... He pushed the long-locked-away memories down. There had been a very good reason why he had gone into family law. But, dammit, his reasons were his own, and they weren't to be talked about or brought up with anyone. Even when the world was falling apart and the wolves were howling at the door, he had to be strong and show no weakness. That was when disaster could strike and everything he'd built could come down around him.

"No. I loved those kids from the day I got to bring them home, and I think they knew that. With Rosie it happened faster because she heard Eric." Newton smiled. "I can complain about a few things, but I wouldn't change my decision for anything." He went around to the passenger side of Chase's BMW and got in, while Chase slid into the plush driver's seat. "I always wanted one of these." A cloud passed over Newton's expression.

"Before you had kids?" Chase supplied as he started the engine, and it purred to life. Or maybe it was before whatever had happened to his leg. Chase was curious, but he didn't want to ask in case he came off as silly. He was pretty sure people asked Newton about his leg all the time, and it was really none of his business. And if he were honest, it wasn't a big thing. To Chase it meant that Newton had been through something pretty difficult and survived to come out the other side. That in itself was pretty cool.

Newton nodded. "Before a lot of things." He sat back, and once they were both belted in, Chase pulled away from the curb. "I promise not to talk about the kids all night."

Chase couldn't help laughing. "It's okay. I asked you to dinner because you interested me, and the kids are part of who you are." There was something about Newton as a parent that Chase found attractive. Maybe it was his nurturing nature and that Chase hadn't had that sort of influence in his life in quite some time. It was difficult for him to tell.

Newton narrowed his gaze. "Doesn't the age difference give you pause?"

Chase shrugged. Honestly, he hadn't given it any thought. "You aren't that much older than I am." He glanced at Newton, noticing the thin lines around his eyes and the light color at his temples for the first time. The fact that Newton was older than he was had barely registered.

"I'm forty-two," Newton said.

"And I'm twenty-nine, though I feel like I'm going on fifty sometimes." Chase pulled to a stop at the sign and then continued on. "My best friend Drake says that life begins at thirty. Though he said that same thing about twenty-five. He changes with every milestone he reaches." Drake was a stitch most of the time. "But I never gave much thought about things like that. I'm younger than a lot of the people I work with and many of my clients." He didn't want this to be an issue. "Is it a problem for you?"

"No. It just surprised me that a guy like you, with so much energy and vitality, would show any interest in someone as old and...." Newton stopped. "How about we forget it? This is just my own insecurities and ridiculousness taking over. You asked me out for a nice dinner, and I don't mean to bring down the conversation." He shifted slightly in his seat, seemingly trying to get comfortable. "What do you do for fun?"

"I'm trying to make partner. There isn't a lot of time for fun. Since I graduated from law school and joined the firm, I've been working at least sixty hours a week. There are clients to meet, documents to create, billing to facilitate, and then court and hearing time, which can be so danged slow. Very little starts on time— unless you're stuck in traffic, and then everything runs exactly on schedule... except you." Chase smiled. "I'm never late for court because I always leave earlier than I think I need to, but I have cut it close a few times, and there is nothing worse than standing in a hearing sweating like a pig." He chuckled. "Though the second time that happened, the other attorney thought I was nervous, but I ended up wiping the floor with him."

"Is that how things work?"

"Yeah. It's an adversarial system to a large degree. You make your argument and do your best to poke holes in the other side. I like to think I'm very good at it."

"Angela certainly thinks so. She was singing your praises when I talked to her today." Newton glanced out the window as they zipped down the freeway toward downtown Milwaukee. "I really appreciate you helping her. It meant a great deal to her and to me." Newton grew quiet, and Chase figured there was something he wanted to say and was hesitating. "I wish I could get attorneys like you for more of my clients. So many of them are lost in a bureaucratic nightmare of denied benefits and delays that cause them grief on top of hurt."

"Newton... I...." There was no way he could take on any more clients for Newton. Not with Milton looking at him so closely.

"I wasn't asking you to take on any more. I know you aren't able to, and it isn't fair of me, but I wanted to let you know that I really appreciate what you did." The smile Newton sent his way was radiant, and Chase basked in its glow for a second, keeping his attention on the road. "Where are we going?"

"There's a great place called Lincoln's near my building. They opened a month ago. It's been popular for lunch, and the food is amazing. I helped the owner with all the paperwork and licensing that was required, so they owe me a few favors." Chase made the turn off the freeway, and they spent some time in stop-and-go surface traffic before pulling up to a converted Third Ward storefront that had been given new life with a redesign and amazing lighting.

He found a place to park, then came around to Newton's side of the car to open the door for him while he got out. It took him a few seconds to unwind his legs, and he winced as he took the first few steps.

"Sometimes it seizes up on me." Newton leaned more heavily on his cane, and Chase held the door open for him. The interior space was rich and warm. They had kept the original woodwork of the building, using paint to brighten up the rest of the space.

The hostess greeted Chase by name. "How are you? It's been a few weeks."

"I'm well, Charlene, and you?" He smiled and introduced Newton briefly. "I'd like one of the more private tables. I called Garth and told him we were coming. He said he would prepare something special for us." He handed her a tip and thanked her for her help. Charlene smiled, and Chase knew she'd make sure they were well taken care of.

Chase waited until Newton was seated before taking his own place. "I really hope you like Italian. This area of town was an old Italian neighborhood, and when Garth opened the restaurant, he worked with the local community to develop dishes that reminded them of home. You won't find pizza on his menu, but you will find Roman and Tuscan staples, such as Amatriciana and carbonara. Though he's put his spin on each dish. I did ask him for his version of Tuscan steak, so we'll see what he comes up with."

"That sounds lovely."

Chase leaned over the table. "I wasn't sure if you ate seafood or had allergies yourself."

"There are things I have to be careful of." Newton chewed his bottom lip. "I can't eat eggplant, and I have to be careful of dairy to a degree." He wiped his eyes and turned toward the kitchen, putting his napkin over his mouth. A strong scent wafted into the dining room and then dissipated quickly. Newton excused himself, making for the restroom as quickly as he seemed to be able to move. Chase wondered what that was about, but shrugged it off as Newton needing to go.

The server stopped at the table, and Chase asked him to come back in a few minutes, watching for Newton. When he returned, he seemed pale, and his right hand shook a little.

"Are you all right?" Chase stood when Newton approached. He seemed unsteady on his feet, and Chase steadied him until he sat back down.

"I will be." Newton sipped his water and appeared to be working to try to get himself under control. Chase didn't understand why

Newton was acting this way, and he ran through their conversation in his head, trying to think if there was anything he'd said that would have upset him. But nothing came to mind. "I'm okay." Newton smiled and took another drink of water.

"If you're sure," Chase said, and sat down again. "If it's the food, we can go somewhere else or just order off the menu."

"No," Newton countered quickly. "The dinner you described sounds heavenly. I eat way too many chicken nuggets and mac and cheese. I've been looking forward to this since you asked." He smiled and let out a deep breath.

The server took their drink orders, and by the time he left, Newton's color seemed better. "Where did you go to school?"

"I went to law school at UW–Madison. I used to watch reruns of shows like *LA Law* and thought it would be fun to be a lawyer. I was able to argue anything when I was a kid, so I figured I would be good at it. I was recruited by Howard and Lickman right out of college. They were a top firm in the state with a great reputation for excellence. We've been able to grow quite a bit in the last four years. We didn't have anyone who practiced family law before I joined the firm, but now it's becoming more and more lucrative for us."

"Is that what you always wanted to do?"

Chase shrugged. "I wanted to help people. Most of my classmates gravitated toward corporate law because that's where they thought the money was. I went where my heart seemed to lead me, and I really love it. I get to help people like Angela and my other clients through some of the toughest times of their lives. Divorce is ugly, really ugly, but custody fights and…." He was going down a road he didn't want to travel.

"You try to do what's best for the children," Newton supplied, to Chase's gratitude.

"Yes. But I don't always get to choose the side I'm on. I have represented people I know are completely despicable, and I have to present their case to the best of my ability. That part of my job pretty much sucks." He paused while the server brought their sodas. They had each ordered a Diet Coke. "They teach us that in law school, but it isn't until we get out into practice that we really come to understand what it means." He rarely got to choose the clients he received. That was often done by the firm, so there had been times when he'd found himself on what he thought was the "wrong" side of a case.

"I can see that. I don't get to pick the people I work with either. Part of my job is to try to weed out those people who are trying to game the system or get benefits they aren't entitled to. Mostly I work with families and as an advocate for the children. They're the most important and often overlooked piece in this puzzle."

"Chase!" Garth said as he came over to the table. He was a large man, like he'd eaten a lot of his own cooking, with a jolly face and intense eyes. The man loved to cook and took it seriously. "You made it."

"Yes. Thanks for finding a place for us." He greeted him with a warm handclasp. "This is Newton," Chase said.

Newton nodded and shook hands with Garth. "I'm really looking forward to dinner. Chase has said you're doing something special."

Garth clapped his hands in delight. "Oh yes. The first course is coming out in just a minute. A few antipasti and then some pasta. I've made a version of Amatriciana with a little kick, and then I have a steak that I got today. It's gorgeous, and I'm going to cook it Florentine-style. You will love it." He looked at both their glasses. "You sure you don't want some wine?"

"I'm driving." Chase turned to Newton. "You feel free if you'd like some."

"I don't drink." The words seemed forced. "But thank you." The paleness had returned, and Chase thought he had a pretty good idea what was going on.

"I appreciate you doing this for me."

Garth grinned. "Anytime. You helped make all this possible." He motioned all around the room, which had filled up even more since their arrival. "We are booked solid on weekends and most nights." It seemed he was really making a success of the place. "I need to get to the kitchen, but I will be back to check on the food and see how delighted your taste buds are." He breezed away with unexpected grace for a guy of his size.

"He's something else," Newton said.

"You better believe it. He and I were in the same dorm freshman and sophomore year. It wasn't for him, so he left college and went to culinary school. It's where his passion was—still is. The man is a genius with food." Chase leaned over the table. "And he says he owes it all to his grandmother. She was the one who first taught him to cook."

The plate of appetizers arrived: olives, prosciutto, salami, peppers. It was amazing, as it always was, and Newton really appeared to enjoy it. After they had finished that course, Newton exchanged a few texts with his sitter and seemed happy.

"They're doing fine. Eric is so incredibly active, but we have to be careful after one of his attacks. So he's under strict orders to rest and stay still, not that he's likely to have much energy for another day or so. I got him some Lego building sets, some of the larger ones where he has to read the instructions step by step in order to put it together. The sitter told me he's done one completely and is working on the second one."

"That's good, isn't it?" Chase asked.

Newton chuckled. "God, yes. It's something other than running around the house like a banshee or sitting in front of a video game. He has some reading and comprehension issues that we're working on." He rolled his eyes. "I'm sorry. I didn't mean to turn the conversation back to the kids." He sipped his soda. "It's just that they're what my life revolves around when I'm not at work. I used to garden and spend a lot of time in the yard, but now I'm lucky if I can get it mowed so it doesn't look like a hayfield. If I can keep the house somewhat clean and the yard from looking like it's something out of Fright Night, then I think I'm doing pretty okay."

"You're doing a great job as far as I can see. The kids are happy, and the house is clean to my eyes. No one is being hurt, and you seem pretty happy yourself." Chase snagged the last olive, munching on the sharp deliciousness. "Sometimes it's a matter of priorities." That was the story of his life. Chase knew he could never do all the things he wanted, so he prioritized.

"What are yours?" Newton asked.

"Making partner in the firm. Associates work hard for years to try to catch the attention of the partners and have a shot at being offered a position on the letterhead. I wanted to do it before I was thirty, and I might make it." Chase leaned over the table. "There's a big case that I'm meeting for tomorrow morning, and Milton, the senior partner, hinted that if it goes well, this could be the one that puts me over the top. Of course, he didn't say that exactly—because we're lawyers, nothing ever gets promised that blatantly in case it can be taken as a contract or something. But I know that's what he meant."

"Will you work less hours if you make partner?" Newton asked.

"A little. One of the things that I'd be able to do is decide on my own cases. I won't have to take those that I don't want or just have them handed to me. It will be a chance to really be my own person and build a legal brand for myself." God, that was what Chase wanted more than anything else: to be the master of his own fate, to a degree at least.

The server brought the house-made pasta, setting the impeccably presented bowls in front of them. The sauce was orangey-red, dotted with bacon, and as soon as Chase took a bite, he understood what Garth was saying. He had added some pepper, and the sauce leapt off the plate, leaving a little residual heat on the tongue.

"Dang, this is good." Newton tucked in like he was starving, and Chase smiled at his gusto.

"When was the last time you ate something you didn't cook?" Chase asked.

"Well… my mother cooks for us when I take the kids to visit, but… things are strained with her. She did her best to understand me being gay, but it's hard for her. She has been a lifelong Jehovah's Witness, so she's had to reconcile her faith and the fact that I'm gay. And I'm sorry to say that it hasn't gone well. She loves her grandchildren, but keeps insisting that I should try to find a woman to settle down with and help me raise Rosie and Eric." Newton took another bite. "Our visits often turn tense, and I sometimes go shopping or find errands to run while the kids spend time with her. We'll have Sunday dinners with her sometimes, and she'll cook, which is nice, and she always sends food home with us." Newton continued eating.

"I know my mom is doing the best she can, but I really wish she'd back off...."

"I guess I'm lucky. My mom was supportive when I came out. I think in a way she was relieved. She had me when she was seventeen, so she isn't much older than you are." Chase wondered what she'd think of Newton. His mom was pretty understanding about most things.

"What about your dad?" Newton asked.

Chase hesitated the same way he always did when asked that question. So many of his dealings with the man who had fathered him were mixed up and turned around. "I don't have anything to do with him," he answered. Hating this subject, but figuring he should get it out of the way. "The last time I saw him was when I was ten. Mom and I did okay together, and I can live with that." He took another bite of the pasta, but the liveliness had gone out of the dish. "Okay. I think that's a long enough trip down Maudlin Road. Let's change the subject. What sort of music do you like?"

Newton's expression brightened. "I love to listen to all kinds. The kids and I sometimes have dance parties. They dance, and I stand and rock as best I can. They love the music from *Descendants*, and Rosie will bop around the room to the music. Of course they like good old-fashioned rock 'n' roll as well. I hope that one of them will take up music in some way. I'd get them any instruments or lessons they want. I wish I'd had the opportunity to play an instrument."

"You didn't?" Chase asked. "I had piano lessons for eight years. I used to dream about playing on the stage at Carnegie Hall. That stage, and just a piano and me." He sighed as his mind took him back to those daydreams.

"Why didn't you go for it?"

Chase finished the last of his pasta and set his fork down. "My mom helped me a great deal after... well, after Dad was gone. She put a lot of things on hold, and when I realized the chances of me making it big in that line of work—and the fact that I could argue a tree out of its bark—I went to law school."

"Do you still play?"

Chase nodded. "I have a piano at home. It was one of the things I bought for myself when I got one of my bonuses. I really wanted to be able to play again. And I think it helps center me." It felt a little strange to be talking this much about himself, and yet right at the same time. "When I'm having trouble with a case or just can't seem to get a handle on what I should do, I sit at the piano and let my fingers go where they want. It's one of the few times that my mind will quiet and I can be alone with myself."

"Music is what I turn to when I'm upset. I put on some opera or a symphony after the kids have gone to sleep and sit in the room, letting the music surround me. My job is stressful either because I have more cases than I can handle, or there are things I'd like to be able to do to help and I can't. A lot of times there just aren't enough resources to go around. I had a family six months ago who needed a place to live, but because of some technicality, I couldn't place them." Newton slapped the table slightly. "She was out on her own and trying to get away from her husband, but hadn't filed yet, so we had to take his income into consideration, even though he was refusing to give her anything."

"Did she get a court order to make him pay?"

Newton shrugged. "I don't know. I couldn't help, and she fell off the radar." He gripped the edge of the table. "I hope her family stepped in. It's impossible to track everyone all the time, especially when they stop asking for help."

Chase understood that clearly. "Sometimes people show up in my office, but never pursue their case for whatever reason. I can't take every case that crosses my desk, no matter how much I might want to." He raised his gaze, meeting Newton's gorgeous brown eyes as their server brought a slab of wood with a huge sizzling steak on top. He didn't look away for a few seconds, loving being the center of the warm attention.

Garth set the side dishes on the table and stepped back. Their server had already stepped away. "Dang, you two," he said softly. "I sort of figured this was a date, but this table is as hot as my kitchen." He smiled, and Chase tried not to roll his eyes.

Newton sat straighter and turned to Garth. "You're a naughty man. I like it." His smile was radiant with a touch of mischief, and when he turned to him, Chase had to stop himself from pulling on his shirt as the temperature in the room rose by a good ten degrees.

"Chase, this man is a keeper." Garth took a large knife and cut the steak into strips across the grain, then filled their plates before wishing them a good meal and leaving the table.

"The potatoes are marvelous, with the herbs and olive oil," Newton said, reaching for his phone when it vibrated. He paled and slid away from the table a little, making a call. "Yes?" He listened quietly, growing more tense. "Give him some water and let him eat the potato chips. With the episode he had a few days ago, we need to keep his sodium levels up." Some of the worry shifted out of Newton's shoulders.

Chase wanted to stand and go up behind him, to massage his taut muscles, but that wasn't something he could do here.

"Can I talk to Eric?" Newton drew his chair nearer to the table. Eric must have come on the phone. "Did you have a good time? ... And you're home now? ... Are you feeling okay? Remember, you aren't to bend down, and you need to stay settled. Have you been drinking water every hour like I told you?" He smiled. "Good. Now have the chips that I set aside for you, and make sure you have your pillows on the bed so you're sitting up a little. And when I get home, I'll come up and say good night, I promise." He chuckled, and then Rosie must have come on. He soothed her and said good night, once again promising to say good night when he got home. Then he hung up with a grin.

"Is Eric okay?" Chase asked between bites. Those two kids had really gotten to him. Even when he'd been hurting, Eric hadn't fussed or complained... well, not too much at any rate. He'd sat in the back seat, scared and worn out, waiting while Newton did his best to keep him calm. And the way little Rosie had snapped into action, brought the bag, probably as she'd done before—what a sweetheart.

"He's fine. Eric wanted the chips, and the sitter wasn't so sure. I should have been more specific with her." He set his phone to the side and slowly cut a piece of steak, then hummed as he chewed. Damn, that sound zinged up Chase's spine. It was sensuous and sexy.

He took his own bite, enjoying the sear and the seasoning. Garth did an amazing steak, and the rest of the meal was quintessentially Italian without being… predictable. It all had zip and an extra spice that was all Garth. He took classic Italian dishes and made them his own, which made them special.

"I just worry, especially after one of his episodes. I'm probably overprotective." Newton returned to eating, and their conversation died away a little. Which was okay.

"Have you dated a lot?" Chase asked as he started to get full and figured Newton had to be as well. They had nearly polished off the beef and the potatoes, along with the grilled vegetables.

"Not really. Before I adopted Rosie, one of my coworkers decided that I needed to get out of the house and away from Eric for a while. So she fixed me up with a friend of hers. Apparently she thought he and I would get along." Newton rolled his eyes dramatically.

"Things crashed and burned?" Chase asked, amused at Newton's grimace.

"Nuclear." Newton groaned. "He wasn't a good fit at all. The guy hated kids. When he came to the house and Eric hurried to the door with me, he took a step back and nearly fell off the stoop. The sitter hadn't arrived yet, so I asked him to sit down. Eric climbed onto the sofa next to him and started talking. The kid isn't shy— never has been. I went to get my date something to drink, and by the time I came back, Stone looked as though he wanted to coat both himself and Eric in Purell." Newton actually smiled and then chuckled. "When I look back on it now, it's funny, but at time, I didn't know how to deal with it. Stone was really handsome and smoldering hot. So we waited for the sitter, and I went out with him." He drank some soda and shook his head. "What a mistake that was. Stone made a reservation at an expensive restaurant… you know, the kind with high prices and almost no food. He drank nearly as much as he ate, and then after the meal, he got a call and had to rush away…."

"The bastard stuck you with the check?" Chase's eyes widened. "What a slime."

"Yup. Took half the grocery money for the week to pay it. Then I had to call a friend to take me home because he had insisted on driving." Newton shook his head. "Stone actually had the guts to call me the next day, apologizing and completely not understanding why I wasn't interested in having another 'go' with him." He leaned over the table. "I think the guy might have had a cane fetish of some kind. I'm not really sure." He winked.

Chase coughed as he tried to laugh. "Most likely he was just a clueless jerk. What did your colleague say when you told her?"

Newton's expression grew serious. "She shrugged and offered to fix me up with another friend. I declined." He remained serious for a second, then burst out laughing. "That's the truth. She tried to fix me up again. I figured once was more than enough."

"It sounds like it." Chase sat back in his chair. "I promise I won't stick you with the check or leave you stranded."

"Then that will make this the best date I've had in ten years," Newton quipped, and they shared a smile.

Chase wondered if that could be true. Was this only the second date Newton had had in all that time? It seemed inconceivable to him.

"How about you?"

"I've gone out a few times, but nothing was ever serious. Most of the guys I dated were interested in sex, which is fine, but I didn't have time for much more than that. And then there were the guys who wanted to settle down and get married."

"You don't want that?" Newton asked.

"Guess I never really gave it a lot of thought. I've been working so hard for so long… and at the time, settling down and putting the kind of effort into a relationship that they required wasn't something I could do."

"And can you now?" Newton pushed his chair back and reached down. Chase leaned to the side, watching as Newton rubbed his leg. Chase got to his feet and pulled out the other chair, then helped Newton put his foot on it. Newton stretched out with a soft sigh. "Thank you. That helps." He drank some water.

"To answer your question, I don't know. I've been alone for a long time, but I've never been really good at relationships. I can do hookups, and I dated guys in college and stuff. But I was always too driven, and they all told me eventually that they were never going to be first in my life because I was in a relationship with my studies or my job and there was no room for them." Chase shrugged, trying to pass it off as unimportant. But coming home to an empty house each night was getting boring. He didn't have a lot of friends because he had never really taken the time to cultivate any. "I know how it sounds." Even to his own ears, it sounded sad and rather stupid.

Newton's reaction wasn't what he was expecting. He actually smiled. "You're a turtle. I never would have guessed that about you after seeing you in court the other day. You threw yourself into the case and seemed so animated. But when things get tough or you need to protect yourself, you pull into your shell."

"Excuse me?" Chase asked.

"There's nothing bad about it. But think about it. You've hinted a couple times that something bad happened to you… and your dad was probably the culprit. So you've pulled inward."

Chase wasn't sure he liked that analogy.

"I'm not being critical. See, I'm a turtle too." Newton raised his eyebrows rather seductively.

"I know you hurt your leg, but why the turtle thing? I understand mine. I have trouble trusting people. I bet you could figure that out pretty easily."

"Yeah… well… there are lots of reasons. The biggest one is that…." He swallowed and shook his head. "I can't talk about it. This is a first date, and you don't need to hear about all that. It would take the rest of the evening, and I'd much rather talk about something else more pleasant. Like my last root canal."

"That bad?" Chase asked teasingly. "So what would you like to talk about? Favorite movies? I love action movies and old films. I was watching the original movie *M*A*S*H* the other day. I didn't remember how funny it was until I saw it as an adult."

"Yeah. I love that too. I like musicals so I can sing along. Though Eric and Rosie tell me that I can't sing for crap and put their hands over their ears when I do." Newton grinned. "That's half the reason I sing, just to get a rise out of those two stinkers. I watched the original *Sunset Boulevard*, and man was it campy and intense at the same time."

"I love that movie," Chase said, his excitement rising. "All right, Mr. DeMille, I'm ready for my close-up." He mugged for Newton, who laughed.

Their server brought the check, and Chase handed him his credit card without looking at it. "Garth makes a great tiramisu, but if you want dessert, I thought we could go to Kopp's. They have mint chip frozen custard as the flavor of the day, and I love that stuff." He signed the check when the server returned.

"Sounds good. I don't care for their food, but I could get some custard to go for the kids tomorrow." Newton grabbed his cane from the back of the chair and used it to stand, then walked slowly toward the door.

"Does your foot hurt all the time?" Chase asked once they had stepped outside.

"Pretty much. There isn't anything they can do about it. At first they thought I was going to lose it. Sometimes I wonder if it would have been better if they had removed it. I could have a prosthetic and it wouldn't hurt so much. But at the very least it's still mine." Newton stopped. "I hate talking about it because everyone doesn't need to hear me whine."

Chase checked his watch. "I've been with you for three hours now. You've mentioned it twice, and neither time did you whine." He came closer, putting an arm around Newton's shoulder. "I'd like to hear what happened sometime when you feel like talking." Of course that meant he'd have to explain to Newton what had happened to him. But then maybe that wasn't so bad. To his surprise, the idea didn't fill him with dread the way talking about his past usually did. He could trust Newton with his hurt.

"That's a deal. Now how about some of this frozen custard you promised me?" Newton said.

Chase led Newton to the car, drove back toward his home, pulled off at Silver Spring Drive, and headed down to the frozen custard stand. "Is your foot okay? I can get the custard and we can eat it in the car," Chase offered.

"I'd love you forever." Newton sighed.

Chase lowered the windows and hurried inside. He had to wait in line, but he didn't mind. Chase liked doing things for Newton.

Maybe it was because it seemed Newton was the one doing things for everyone else and Chase thought it was time someone helped him. But more likely it was the smile that went all the way to his eyes that Chase received as he approached the car with two dishes of mint chocolate chip that smelled as heavenly as it tasted.

Chase slipped into his seat, handed Newton his dish, and stifled a groan at the enticing sounds Newton made as he ate. "I know the custard is good, but are you eating it or making love to that spoon?" He had to tease at the little hums of delight that sent a wave of heat strong enough to melt the frozen treat in seconds racing through him. More than once tonight, Chase had wondered if Newton would make those same sounds in bed. God, he wanted to find out.

"Smartass," Newton retorted, and snickered. "I never get to swear anymore."

"I get the feeling there are a lot of things you don't get to do." Chase set his dish on the dash and leaned over the seat. "You have a little chocolate on your lip."

"Where?" Newton reached for the mirror, but Chase stopped him with a touch.

"I'll get it." He leaned closer, touching Newton's lips with his. Mint and chocolate mixed with the heady taste of Newton, all of it bursting on his tongue as he kissed him. Then he backed away. "See, now you're much better." Damn, Chase loved kissing Newton, with his wide eyes and the way his lips parted.

Newton stared at him as though he were shocked. "You kissed me."

"Is that bad? Do you want me to stop? I can take it back." Chase winked and leaned closer once again. "You taste thrilling." For a second he was worried he'd read the situation all wrong. Then Newton smiled, and Chase drew in once again. "Can I have some more?" Frozen custard be damned—*this* was really worth the trip.

This time Newton took the initiative, and they ended up making out like teenagers for a few minutes. Their custard had melted by the time they returned to it, not that either of them seemed to mind. Chase took care of the trash, and hurried inside, got some custard to go, and happily started the engine before backing out of the parking space, driving to Newton's, and parking in front of his house. He kissed Newton good night in the car, then walked him to the door and gave him the treat for the kids. Then he stayed until Newton went inside before returning to his car.

CHAPTER 3

"How are your little darlings?" Jolene asked from across the lunch table a week later. "We work in the same office and yet we haven't had a chance to talk much." She was a close friend and one of his parenting partners. Newton hadn't really thought a great deal about being a parent before he'd met Eric and made the decision to foster and eventually adopt him. Jolene had a son about Rosie's age, as well as a nine-year-old daughter, and lived a block from him, so they'd quickly become friends, and she was his go-to person for parenting advice.

"They're growing up fast. How are Kirsten and Stevie doing?"

"The same as yours, I suppose. Kirsten has decided that she's old enough that she doesn't need a mother, until she does. And she never stops moving. I swear, she has so much energy. In my case, it's Stevie who's the quiet one. He'd spend all day sitting on my lap or next to me as long as I was reading him a story. He asked me last week to teach him how to read so he could tell himself stories." She grinned. "He said I don't do the voices right anymore and he can do them better in his own head."

Newton laughed out loud, a few people turning to look at them in the downtown café. "What does Hayden think of all this?"

"That man loves his kids. We're going on vacation in a month, and he has activities planned for each and every day while we're out in Colorado. Hiking, visiting all kinds of roadside attractions, the drive to the top Pikes Peak. All of it." She smiled. "There are times when I think I'm completely secondary." She sipped her coffee. "He'll spend hours with the kids, and there are times I can't seem to get his attention at all." She sighed. "Then he'll come home with flowers and everything changes."

"What did he want with the flowers?" Newton winked, and Jolene nodded.

"Well, *that*, but there was this contest at work for selling so many cars, and he more than met his goals, so he got to choose the prize he could take. One was a new set of golf clubs, and I know Hayden had been looking at them the entire time. They were just what he's been eyeing for years now." She laid her hand on the table. "But look...." The diamond tennis bracelet sparkled on her wrist. "He chose this for me instead. Hayden said he didn't need the new clubs that badly." She practically glowed when she talked.

"I guess he does see you," Newton said.

"Yes. He does, and as more than just the mother of his children. I know I'm being stupid, but sometimes I feel like that's all I am. Part of the prize from work is a weekend at the Renaissance in Chicago, though. My parents are going to come stay with the kids so Hayden and I can have two days away." She practically vibrated with excitement. "But that's enough about me. If you think I asked you to lunch so we could talk about me and Hayden, you're crazy." She waggled her eyebrows. "When I called the house to talk to you, Eric said you went on a date."

"I had dinner with a new friend I met through work," Newton clarified.

"Uh-huh. You do know that your son has his bedroom in the front of the house. He saw you in the car, kissing. So, therefore, it's a date."

"Chase is hot, a lawyer, and we had a good time. Though he and I definitely didn't talk about first date kinds of stuff."

Jolene rolled her eyes. "It's been so long since you went on anything that might resemble a date, I don't think you know what first date conversation should be."

"We talked about the kids, his work, mine a little, music, and movies. Stuff like that. It was a wonderful evening, and Chase was really nice and kept watching me." Newton shivered as he remembered the intensity of some of those gazes. "But he's a lawyer, and even he said he was too busy for a relationship. He and I went out to dinner... that was all. And it's been a week and he hasn't called."

"Has he texted?" Jolene asked pointedly.

"Yes. A few times. But he's never mentioned us going out again. They're only general texts and stuff." Which he kept saved in his phone, each and every one of them.

Jolene shook her head. "Chase asked you out to dinner, right? And he's texted you and kept in touch. Did it ever occur to you that he was waiting for you to ask him out this time? You can't expect Chase to do all the work and show all the interest. If you aren't going to ask him out or make a move of some kind, why should he?"

The notion had never occurred to Newton. "So I should ask him out?"

"Do you know what you want? Do you like this guy?" Jolene asked, staring at him until Newton grew uncomfortable and looked away first. "You do?"

"What's not to like? He's hot and really sexy. Watching him work in court was like watching an artist at work. He threw himself into what he was doing, and he was willing to help a client of mine for free. I think he has a good heart." Newton wasn't willing to trust him with any of his secrets yet, but he was convinced that Chase was a caring person. "But there's pain in his past."

"And you have plenty of that in yours. What's the problem?" She shrugged. "Shared pain is eased pain. That's what my gran used to say. If you want to lessen the burdens you carry inside, the only way is to share them with someone else." She sipped her coffee, and Newton wondered if she could be right. "And please, not me. I already know most of your secrets." She patted his hand.

"Are you going to give me the lecture on how I need to find someone to share my life with, that you're worried about the amount of time I'm alone… or some such rubbish?" he asked.

Jolene shook her head. "Nope. I don't have to. I'd say your mother has already done a pretty good job of that. I'm willing to bet that you've heard that plenty from her over the years. Of course, your mother is probably more like 'You need to find a wife.'" Jolene rolled her eyes. "Sometimes I think that woman is totally blind. How she can't know and understand what it means to be gay is beyond me."

Newton shrugged. It was an old argument, and one that wasn't going to change. She had her faith, and that had seen his mother through some very difficult times for her. Newton didn't really blame her for holding on the way she did. He knew better than most that everyone needed some comfort in their lives, and who was he to deny his mother hers? He simply wished that she didn't try to foist her beliefs and worldview on everyone else. Still, his mother loved him in her own way, and she adored the kids, so that was all he really could ask for.

"Mom is who she is. It isn't fair to expect anything else." Newton wasn't going to expend any more energy on what he could do nothing about.

"You're a better person than I am," Jolene said. "Still, maybe your mother is right, and you need to put yourself out there. Eric and Rosie are going to grow up, and with each passing year, they're going to need you less and less. You deserve someone in your life who's there for you."

"But you complain about Hayden all the time," Newton challenged.

"Yeah, I do. He's my husband, and there are times when the man drives me completely crazy. But he's also there for me whenever I need him, and he has to listen to me when the kids have driven me to distraction. For all his faults, Hayden is a good man, and when it comes down to it, I know that in his life, I come first. And there's something to be said for that. Once everyone is grown and the kids are out of the house, it will be him and me again. Hayden already has plans for some of the things he and I are going to do together. Will they happen? Who knows? But he's already thinking of twenty years down the road... with me. And I like that, knowing he'll still be there and that I'll be there for him."

"But what if something happens and the earth opens up?" *Or buildings fall on top of you?* He didn't say that part, but it was in his mind. "Those plans could come to nothing."

"That could happen anyway. The thing is, Hayden has the dreams and the plans. They'll change over time, but you can't move forward without having them. Otherwise we go in boring circles, wandering in the dark and never really getting where we want to go." She was amazingly smart. It was part of why Newton liked her so much. "What are your dreams? You have to have some."

Newton shrugged. "I guess to get the kids to the point where they're happy, healthy adults. I don't want a lot in life." He leaned to the side as Jolene swiped at him over the table.

"That is so lame. Close your eyes and think of what you really want. What did you see for yourself when you graduated college? We're all idealistic then."

Newton did as she suggested, but no real dreams came to him. "I wanted to help people, and that's what I do every day. And I think I'm pretty good at it."

"Didn't you want more than that? You can't tell me you never dreamed of meeting a hot guy, settling down, and living happily ever after. We all want that."

"Maybe once. There was a time when I used to look up and reach for the stars. I used to wish and dream big. I wanted to make a difference, and I did that—I still do that." He was deliberately being obtuse because he didn't want to think about what he'd lost. "You know there's nothing wrong with keeping your feet on the ground. I have two kids who I love very much, and I want to be able to provide for them. They are going to need braces and college—all that stuff. So I guess that's my dream now." He was pretty pleased until Jolene scoffed, picked up his phone off the table, and shoved it at him.

"You are so danged boring sometimes. Message that hot guy and tell him that you want to take him out. Maybe you could go this weekend. There's a go-cart track out in West Allis—take the kids, see if he wants to go, and for God's sake, have fun." She leaned over the table. "And figure out a way to get yourself some. It's been so long, you have no idea what fun fucking really is." She snickered softly at her joke. "Do you even remember what it's like to have your eyes roll back in your head and to be left breathless by the closeness and intimacy of spending special time with another human being?" She thought a second and sipped her coffee. Then she slid off the stool and grabbed her purse, pulled out her phone, and sent a text.

"What are you doing?" Newton leaned over to try to peek at her phone.

"Sending a dirty message to Hayden. One of us might as well get lucky tonight, and since you won't get off your butt, it might as well be me." She wagged her eyebrows in that way she had and then finished her coffee. "I need to get back, and so do you."

Newton nodded, knowing that his time away from the office was up and that he had plenty waiting for him when he got back. She hugged him once she was ready to go. "I'll see you soon," Newton promised.

Jolene released him. "Think about what I said. You need to have a life of your own." She turned and left the coffee shop, hurrying away down the sidewalk.

Newton checked his phone for the time and did the same. Each step toward the office filled him with indecision. He had a full life right now. Eric demanded a great deal of his attention and energy. His condition meant that Newton had to be on his guard all the time. And Rosie deserved just as much of his attention as Eric received. Between the two of them, they took all his time outside of work.

Newton stopped on the sidewalk, others passing around him like water flowing past a rock in the stream. Maybe Jolene was right after all. He'd spent the last four years giving all his time and energy to Eric and Rosie—not that they didn't deserve it. But he had no one for himself.

Newton tried to think of the last time he had done something purely for himself, and the only thing he could come up with was dinner with Chase. And he spent half the evening talking about the kids. With every topic of discussion, he somehow managed to bring it back to the kids. Man, no wonder Chase hadn't asked him out again. Newton must have been dull as dirt. Still, he was a turtle, Newton knew it, but maybe he'd stayed in his damned shell for way too long. Of course, there was also the fact that Newton was a number of years older than Chase. So maybe Chase was interested in seeing someone his own age.

"When did I get to be such a damned coward?" Newton asked out loud, and a lady on the sidewalk paused to turn to him, squinting as though he were crazy. She moved on, and still Newton parted the flow of people. Then, making his decision, he pulled out his phone and sent Chase a text message asking if he'd like to join them for some fun this Saturday. The kids were the most important part of his life, but if he wanted the chance at something more, something of his own, then they also needed to fit with the rest of what was important to him.

Newton put his phone in his pocket, smiling at himself for taking one small step to poke his head out of his thick, protective shell. Granted, it was a single gesture, but still, he was happy about it, and when his phone vibrated, he pulled it out, surprised to have received such a quick answer.

AFTER WORK that evening, Newton hurried home so he could meet Eric and Rosie as they got off the bus from after-school activities. It was an important ritual, and they were both full of stories about their day as the three of them walked back to the house. Inside, Rosie and Eric went upstairs to change their clothes while Newton answered the ringing house phone.

"Hi, Mom." She was the only person to regularly use that number. She just didn't seem to remember his cell.

"Newton, I thought I'd call and have you over for dinner on Saturday. I'd like to spend some time with my grandchildren." She never phoned because she wanted time with him. Not that he felt too badly about it. If he and his mother spent too much time together, the walls began to feel like they were closing in.

"We have plans on Saturday. We're going to go out with a friend." He didn't go into details.

"A girlfriend?" she asked hopefully. "You know, it's about time you settled down and found someone to be a mother to your kids."

"Mom, I'm not going to go out with a woman. His name is Chase, and I met him a week ago. He likes the kids, and we're going to be out that afternoon. We could come for Sunday dinner if you'd like. Eric and Rosie would love to see you." Okay, so he was piling on a little guilt, but his mother used it plenty, so why couldn't he?

She cleared her throat, which was never good. "You're taking those kids along with you while you go on a date with some man?" She said it like she'd just eaten a mouthful of garbage. "How can you do that? The kids need to be raised in a wholesome environment, not one full of sin and disgust. I could keep quiet when it was just you, but now that you've decided to flaunt your lifestyle in front of them, I won't have it."

"My lifestyle? What are you talking about? I deserve a life of my own, and the kids know Chase. They've met him and they like him. As for flaunting anything, you wouldn't know. So, whatever you're thinking, just let it go." Newton's anger rose. "On second thought, the kids and I are busy this weekend, so maybe we'll come to visit some other time." He was getting tired of his mother foisting her own beliefs on him. Newton had always tried to be understanding.

"This isn't right," she sputtered. "I raised you better than that."

"No, Mom. It isn't right. You deciding how I'm going to live my life and raise my children isn't right. And it isn't going to happen. I'll call you later when I'm not so angry, and when I won't say things I can't take back. You have a good day." He hung up the phone and clenched his teeth to keep from screaming in utter frustration.

His cell phone rang, and Newton checked it before answering. "Hi, Chase." He didn't try to keep the pleasure out of his voice.

"I had a few minutes and thought I'd call. What did you have in mind for Saturday?" There was equal happiness running through the line. "I'll need to work for a few hours in the morning. I just got a big case, and I have a ton of research to do." As soon as he mentioned the case, a darkness came over his tone, and Newton wondered what was causing it, but he couldn't ask. Chase owed his clients confidentiality, the same courtesy he had shown to Angela.

"I thought we'd go to lunch, and then Eric has been asking to go to the go-cart track for a month now. It's a full-on fun center, with video games and stuff like that as well. We can go after lunch for a few hours."

"How is Eric?"

"Doing okay. There hasn't been a repeat episode, and they have him on a sort of oral IV with saline that he drinks once a day. He doesn't really care for it, but I have to keep him hydrated with enough saline that it helps keep his fluids in balance. Other than being tired for a few days afterward, he's doing very well and back in school." Newton waited as the kids trooped down the stairs, then followed them into the kitchen for a snack.

"Good. I'll call you on Saturday, and we can arrange to meet somewhere. I'm not sure exactly how things will work, but we'll figure it out." Chase said something Newton didn't catch because of the noise around him. "We'll talk soon."

Newton figured he had to take care of work and said goodbye before hanging up.

"Was that Mr. Chase?" Rosie asked.

"They were kissing when they came home last time," Eric pronounced. "I saw them from my room."

"Daddy and Chase, sitting in a tree, k-i-s-s-i-n-g...," Rosie sang.

Newton picked her up, using the counter to steady himself as he tickled her.

"Daddy!" Rosie squealed in delight.

"Go eat your snack and watch television for a few minutes before you do your homework. And be nice," he scolded lightly.

They hurried out of the room, arguing about what to watch until the television went on and then they grew quiet. It was funny, but for the last week, kissing had been on his mind a lot. He was more than a little interested in kissing Chase again.

He got himself something to eat and sat in the living room.

"Do you think Mr. Chase is going to marry Daddy?" Rosie asked. "He's nice."

There was no answer from Eric, not one that Newton could hear at least, from where he sat at his game.

"If they do, which one will wear the white dress?" Rosie asked.

By Saturday morning, Newton wondered if he was going to go out of his mind. Eric was supposed to keep still and rest, but he was so active, and though Newton kept fluids down him, he worried, a lot. Still, he loved when Eric behaved like a normal kid as opposed to when he sat quietly because all of his energy had been sapped away.

"You both need to pick up all the toys and put your things away. We're going to have lunch with Chase, and then he and I have some fun things planned, but we're not going to do any of it if the two of you can't do what you're supposed to." Newton pointed, and both kids trudged into the living room like he'd sentenced them to a fate worse than death. "I mean it," he said louder. "If you want to play, then you need to earn it, and I wasn't the one who dragged out your toys."

He peeked into the room. Rosie had her arms full of toys and practically waddled out of the area and up the stairs. She came back down too quickly. "Sweetheart, you need to put the toys away, not just drop them on your bed." He smiled as she trudged back up the stairs. Eric at least was putting his things away, and when Rosie came back down, she and Eric finished up while Newton used his cane to climb the stairs. He checked Rosie's room and was pleased that she had put things away in a reasonable way.

The doorbell rang as he reached the bottom of the stairs again.

Rosie ran over and pulled the door open before Newton could stop her. "Mr. Chase!"

"Come on in," Newton said, gently moving Rosie out of the way so he could open the door the rest of the way.

Chase stepped inside, wearing jeans and a sweatshirt, carrying a bag. He pulled out a box of Legos and handed it to Eric. "You're going to have to follow the instructions to put this space shuttle together."

Eric beamed as he took the box. "Thank you." He seemed beside himself. "Can I start this right now?"

"How about after we get home?" Newton suggested.

Eric set the box in the family room as Chase handed Rosie a large plastic-wrapped ball.

"An L.O.L. doll!" she squealed.

"You can play with that when we get home, just like Eric's," Newton told Rosie. "Now, what do you say?"

She rushed over to Chase after setting her gift on the coffee table. "Thank you. It's just the one I always wanted." She gave him a hug, and Newton tried not to chuckle. He probably failed.

"Okay, guys. Get your jackets. It could get a little cool as the sun goes down." He waited while they gathered their things. Sometimes leaving was quite a production, and once they were all ready, he got them out of the house and into his car. It took a few minutes more, but they were eventually ready to head to lunch.

"Are we going to McDonald's?" Rosie asked.

"No. I thought we could get Greek food at the gyros place you guys like." Newton turned to Chase. "It's way better than McDonald's." The look on Chase's face when Rosie mentioned McDonald's was priceless. "It seems you're not a fan."

Chase cleared his throat. "I like a Big Mac every once in a while, but Greek sounds way better." He turned to the back seat. "Is that okay with you guys?"

"Yes."

"Yay."

It seemed from the chorus in the back that they were happy, and Chase seemed happy, judging from the smile sent Newton's way. He liked that they were pleased.

The Greek restaurant wasn't far from the house. Once they arrived, Rosie skipped inside, pulling Eric along as he and Chase brought up the rear.

"I love this place," Chase whispered in his ear, and damned if it didn't send a zing up Newton's spine. He closed his eyes, willing himself to calm down. How could something so mundane get him thinking naughty thoughts about what Chase looked like under his jeans and sweatshirt, both of which hugged him like a second skin?

Newton followed Chase inside, lightly chastising himself for the way his gaze centered on his perfect backside. He closed his eyes, forcing his mind onto another track. Newton was with the kids—he needed to remember that.

"What do you want, Rosie Posey?" Chase teased as he lifted her up so she could see better.

"They usually share a gyro platter with fries," Newton explained, and both kids nodded.

"Okay. Let's make that two because I love those." Chase turned, cocking his eyebrows just so.

It hit Newton right there in the restaurant just how young Chase was. Newton leaned on his cane, imagining he could feel the gray hair sprouting on his head.

"Okay, three. Only, mine with the salad." Newton patted his belly.

Chase leaned close enough that only he could hear his breathing. Then Chase patted Newton's belly, those few seconds of contact sending a ripple running through him. "I'd say you have nothing to worry about." Chase didn't move, and Newton stood stock-still. It was like that simple touch had woven a spell around them. It only lasted for a fraction of a second, and then it was gone, with Chase stepping away, placing the food order, and finding out what everyone wanted to drink. Before Newton could protest, Chase had paid for the food and ushered Rosie and Eric to the booth. He slipped in next to Rosie, and Newton sat across from him next to Eric.

"Do you like go-carts?" Chase asked, and Eric was off on how he'd gotten to go there for a birthday party.

"They were so cool. The red one is the fastest, and it's the most fun. So I want that one."

"Do I get my own too?" Rosie asked.

Newton was about to answer when Chase nudged her. "I thought you could be my copilot. Together we'll show this whippersnapper what fast really is." He smiled at Rosie, and Newton found his chest warming. How could he not like someone who seemed to like his kids?

A server brought their trays of food and set them on the table. Newton thanked him and divided up the food for the kids, who immediately started eating. Over the table, Chase caught his eye, and their gazes locked. Newton paused with his hand on his plate, just watching Chase, getting lost in those blue-gray eyes for a few seconds.

"Dad," Eric said, and he came back to himself, taking his plate and blushing slightly. "You can make goo-goo eyes at Mr. Chase later."

Rosie giggled, and Eric snickered. The comment wouldn't have been so bad if it hadn't been true.

"You kissed daddy," Rosie said.

Newton felt his cheeks heat even more. "There are no secrets at all with kids around." He reached over, tickling Eric. "Especially mine."

"Dad, I'm gonna woof," Eric groused with a smile on his face.

"No woofing. Now, both of you eat your lunch and no teasing Chase or me. It isn't very nice." Newton started eating.

"Maybe, but you're cute when you blush," Chase said.

Newton didn't see how the kids reacted as he stared at Chase, his Cheshire cat grin once again making Newton think of things he knew he shouldn't.

Rosie and Eric were hungry, so as soon as they started eating, they grew quiet.

"How was work? You said you had a new case."

"Yes. It's a big one. At least as big as family law gets. This case has the chance to set a new precedent as far as child custody. But I can't talk about it much because of privacy concerns for the clients, as well as their children. However, this case could make my career on a state and maybe national level. And if it turns out well, cement my bid for partner." Chase smiled and was almost as excited as the kids.

"Is that why you were working?"

"There's a tight time crunch, and I need to be absolutely prepared." Chase ate his gyro, and Newton took a bite of salad. They were having a great day so far, and Newton basked in the shared glow of Chase's attention.

"ARE YOU all done?" Chase asked a while later as he gathered up the debris of lunch onto the trays. Then he threw it all away, took Rosie's hand, and led her out to the car. Eric followed, and Newton made sure the kids hadn't left anything behind before heading out.

They played car games and sang songs on their way across town to the mostly indoor fun center. There were games inside, but they also had a go-cart track that wound around part of the building. By the time he pulled into the parking lot, Eric was talking nonstop about all the things he wanted to do, and Rosie was nearly as wound up as Eric.

"There's a bouncy castle!" Chase sounded just like one of the kids, especially when they all joined in the cry.

Newton paid for go-cart rides and time in the bouncy castle that had been set up on the lawn for all three of them. It seemed it was big enough that Chase could go with them, and he played with Eric and Rosie, who seemed to love having him in with them. Newton stood just outside, leaning on his cane, watching and wishing things were different.

"I know just how you feel," a woman said from the table nearby. She stood with difficulty, very pregnant and looking more than a little uncomfortable. "Blake asked on the way over if I'd go in the bouncy castle with him." She turned her gaze down to her belly. "He doesn't seem to understand that I can't do all the things I could even a few months ago." She smiled and motioned to a seat at her table. Newton joined her, relieved to get off his foot.

"Rosie and Eric have always known me like this. So they understand there are limits. Doesn't help when they're sick and Rosie wants nothing more than to be picked up and comforted and I can't do it." He suddenly felt a wave of wishing. He wanted things to be different so he could do all the things other parents did. He wanted to be able to play with them in a more active way, and he wanted to run and keep up with them, but that wasn't going to happen.

"Your husband looks like he can," she said.

"Chase isn't my husband. This is sort of a second date, I guess." Newton turned to where they were bouncing, Chase holding Rosie's hand, all three of them laughing and having a great time. And that brought up another thing. How was he supposed to keep up with someone young, vital, and whole like Chase? Newton hadn't been whole for a long time. That had been taken from him in a matter of a few hours that had not only changed the world, but the rest of his day-to-day life. He had to push that away. A fun day out with his kids and Chase was not the time for him to dwell on all that. But sometimes he had very little choice when his head decided to mull that shit over.

"He's sure good with them."

Chase smiled and waved at him before climbing out. He stuck his head back inside and then put his shoes on and joined him at the table. "I checked with Eric, and he says he's doing fine. I think we should have him drink something once he comes out, though. That takes a lot more energy than it looks." He reached across the table. "I'm Chase."

"Annabeth," the lady said as she shook his hand. "The other one in there is mine. He'll go until he collapses and falls asleep. I bring him here every couple of weeks, and all he wants is to go in the bounce house, as he calls it. He'd stay in there for an hour if they let him."

"I told the kids five minutes," Chase explained.

"Thanks." Newton smiled and inhaled deeply.

A burning scent tickled the back of his nose. He closed his eyes to try to push it away, but he was back in Lower Manhattan, the screams around him now holding terror as the very earth under him shook, his ears filling with a rumble that went on and on, coming from every direction imaginable. Dust billowed from everywhere, filling his mouth and nose. Instinctively Newton took cover, pressing to the floor, covering his head with his hands, mentally saying a prayer for this hell to end. It went on and on, more and more dust piling on top of him, the entire world shaking, being turned upside down and inside out. Then there was nothing but the screaming, sound on top of sound, building in on itself until it burned out and grew quiet, only to start again and again, over and over until he thought he was going to scream himself.

He gasped for air, but only tasted and felt dust and grime everywhere—in his mouth, nose, eyes, on his skin. He needed to get it off him, get it away so he could breathe.

"Newton," a voice called. Maybe someone had come to rescue him. "It's okay. Where are you?"

He coughed, trying to clear his mouth, and opened his eyes. The sun was shining. The clouds of dust were gone. It took him a few moments to realize where he was—under the table, with Eric, Rosie, Chase, and a bunch of strangers peering down at him.

"Daddy," Rosie whimpered, and crawled down next to him to hug him tightly. "It's okay." She cried, and he held her in return, turning onto his side as he tried to make sense of exactly what had happened. It was flashback, a short one, and he'd been right back there, the day the Towers had fallen.

"I'm okay, sweetheart. I'm fine." He kissed her forehead. "I promise. I'm just fine. I need to get up now, okay?" He released her and peered out from under the table.

"Sir, are you all right?" one of the people from the Fun Emporium asked.

"He's okay. It was a flashback," Chase answered, running interference. "He'll need a few minutes, and please get everyone else away. This isn't a spectator event." He took charge when she didn't, and the people dispersed, leaving Newton alone with his family.

"I'm going to need some help getting out." He slid to the edge, and Chase helped him crawl out and get onto his feet. Rosie handed him his cane and then hugged him. Eric did as well, holding him tightly. Newton realized both kids were scared. "Guys, I'm really okay." He met Chase's concerned gaze.

"Should we go?" Chase asked quietly.

"No." Newton took a deep breath and crinkled his nose. "I don't want to disappoint the kids." Using his cane for balance, he slowly walked farther away from the area. "I'll be okay. The burning popcorn took me by surprise and transported me back… to that day." He took another deep breath as the scent finally began to fade. Chase excused himself, and Newton took Rosie's hand. "I got you guys some tokens for the games. Why don't you go and have some fun? I'm going to sit over there near the door." *Where there's some fresh air.*

"Where's Mr. Chase?" Rosie asked just as the man made a reappearance. "Do you want to play games with us?"

"How about you guys have fun while I sit with your dad for a while? Then we can ride the go-carts." Chase took the seat next to him.

"Watch your sister," Newton cautioned Eric, who nodded, and they headed off into the small forest of video games.

"What happened?" Chase asked.

Newton groaned. He deserved an answer. "Burning popcorn smells just like the scent after the Twin Towers fell. That burning, scorched aroma that sticks in your throat and doesn't let go. I wasn't prepared for it, and suddenly I was right back there."

"You slid under that table and went into a crouch position really fast. Is your foot okay?" Chase asked, lifting it onto the seat of the picnic table.

"It's sore, but it always is. Just another thing I can't get away from." Newton sighed softly. "As flashbacks go, this one wasn't so bad. Though it's been a while since I've had one. I've worked with therapists for a long time to help identify what triggers them.

Usually if I can be ready for them or I'm aware there's a trigger, I can either avoid it or be prepared for it, but this came out of the blue. I should have foreseen it, but I didn't." He felt stupid. Newton had probably scared the people here half to death, and he hoped he hadn't been screaming. His throat didn't feel like it, but that happened sometimes.

"You know it's okay. I'm sorry that happened to you, but I understand." Chase took his hand. "I'm here if you want to talk about it."

"This isn't really a good time, and even talking about it is hard." The last time, there had been anger and resentment that had ended in yelling and even some tears. If that happened again, Newton didn't want to experience it in a public place. "See, when I tell what happened, it's like I'm back there, and one trip like that in a day is more than enough."

"Is that what happened to your foot? Were you working in the pile?" Chase asked.

"I wasn't supposed to be, but I did end up there." He swallowed and tried to breathe as memories of that time started to build like a tidal wave on the horizon, drawing closer and threatening to wash him away yet again.

The children approaching pushed those thoughts from his mind.

"Daddy, look what I won," Rosie said happily as she showed him a stuffed penguin.

"How did you do that?" The games were usually rigged so they rarely paid out. Newton was well aware of that.

Eric followed. "She put her token in that machine, and the claw delivered her the stuffed animal." He shrugged and seemed slightly green with envy.

"Okay. How about we all go ride the go-carts?" Newton turned to Chase. "I think it's time we all enjoyed ourselves." The last thing he wanted was to bring the day down. The kids were entitled to have some fun, and he wasn't going to deny them because of his inability to control his own reality. The trauma was seventeen years ago, and still he had problems with smells. He'd thought he was over the flashbacks. It had been over two years since he'd had one.

"Okay. Let's go. Rosie and I will race you and Eric." Chase took her hand, and they hurried over to get in line, hunched together like they were hatching some nefarious plot. It was adorable.

"Are we going to let them beat us?" Newton asked Eric, who was practically jumping out of his skin with excitement. Newton pulled out the tickets and handed them to the attendant. They got in line and took their places in the cars. Eric wanted to drive his own car but was too young, so he rode with Newton. Once everyone was in place, they pulled out and started racing. Chase and Rosie started out in front, but Newton had the slightly faster car, and he passed them on the straightaway, going ahead and pulling away. Eric crowed when they pulled into the station at the end, and even high-fived him.

"Can we go again?" Newton asked, handing the attendant the tickets. "It's going to be a lot easier if I only have to get out of here once." The car was super low to the ground.

The attendant took the tickets, and they went again. This time he and Eric were in front the entire time, but Rosie and Chase were still grinning.

Newton managed to get out of the go-cart, but it took him quite a while. Chase helped him to his feet, and Newton got his cane under him. His foot felt all right, and they went back inside.

"Can we play more games?" Rosie asked, tugging Newton to the machine where she'd won her penguin.

"We can come back again sometime. It's a nice day, and I thought we could get ice cream if you'd like." He wasn't above a little bribery if necessary.

"Can we get french fries instead?" Rosie asked, and Newton groaned.

"If Daddy says it's all right," Chase agreed, and Newton sighed. It looked like they were going to end up at McDonald's one way or another.

"Okay. Then let's go." The kids led the way out to the car.

Chase held back with him, staying close. "If this is getting to be too much, we can go watch a movie or something," he offered.

Newton stopped before he reached the car. "I don't want to ruin the day, and I'm sorry about earlier. It took me by surprise and...." He'd felt very self-conscious for the last hour and was beginning to fear that he'd become the center of attention, with everyone at the fun center watching to see if he was going to go crazy again.

"It's okay. The kids are fine and ready for a snack, and you haven't ruined anything. Stuff happens." Chase took his arm, holding it firmly, wordlessly saying he was here for him. Newton held Chase's arm in return for just a second and then leaned on him to go to the car.

Once he was inside, he started the engine, checking that Rosie and Eric were buckled in, and then he backed out, heading toward the east side of town. "Did you have fun?" Newton asked.

"Yes, Daddy," Rosie said. "Can we go again with Mr. Chase? He's fun."

"Maybe." Newton sure hoped Chase wanted to go out with him again, but after the little display when they arrived, Newton wasn't so sure. Chase had said the right things, but that didn't mean he wasn't going to go running for the hills. "If he wants to." And with those words he put the ball in Chase's court, hoping he returned it. "What was your favorite part?" Newton asked Eric, who seemed quiet, which worried him. "Eric, you need to drink, okay? The cooler is on the floor. Get something out and drink, okay? There's also a juice box for Rosie."

He heard the cooler lid rattle, and Chase turned around to check on them as Newton drove. "Are you feeling okay?"

"Yeah, I think I just need something to drink," Eric answered.

"Okay. But tell us if you don't feel okay, all right?" Chase kept an eye on Eric, and Newton's worry rose as he sped up.

By the time they reached their side of the city, Eric was talking again and seemed more himself. When Newton parked to get their snack, Eric bounded out of the car like he usually did.

"Did we get him in time?" Chase asked.

"I think so. He seems normal." Watching that Eric drank enough and stayed hydrated was nearly a full-time job. "Thank you for helping."

"They're great kids. Nearly as great as their dad." Chase flashed him a smile, and Newton returned it, wishing he didn't feel so damned old. He looked it too, or at least he thought he did. With the cane and his foot, combined with the flashback, he felt so much older than his years.

Chase raced the kids inside, all three of them laughing, and Newton wondered what Chase could ever possibly see in him. Maybe this was just some sort of "daddy" thing and Newton was setting himself up for heartache.

THE KIDS talked about everything, asking Chase all kinds of questions about his job.

"I want to be a lawyer," Eric announced after barraging Chase with questions. "On TV they get all the girls, and that's what I want." He crossed his arms over his chest as though that were the last word on the subject.

Chase chuckled and shook his head. "But I don't get the girls," he teased.

Eric pursed his lips and rolled his eyes like Chase was completely stupid. "You're gay, like Daddy. So you can have the boys. I'll be a lawyer with you, and I can have the girls." Now that was a pronouncement. He went back to finishing his snack, and Chase sat with his hands around his cup of coffee.

"You've been a really good sport about all this today," Newton said.

Chase released his coffee, taking Newton's hand. "I'm smart enough to know that being interested in you means that your kids have to like me too. It isn't only you. It's them too." He gently caressed Newton's fingers.

"They're holding hands," Rosie stage-whispered.

"Just eat your french fries," Newton told her. "You know it's normal for adults to hold hands and things like that when they like each other." Newton turned to both kids. "I like Chase, and I think he likes me. So we may hold hands and things like that. That doesn't mean that I love either of you any less or that I'm going to pay less attention to you." Newton made sure they were both looking at him.

"But you never date," Eric said.

"Yeah. That's true up to now. But is it okay if Chase and I date?" Newton knew it was best to be honest with them and to ask their opinions.

"I like him," Rosie said for her endorsement, and Eric nodded in a "Why ask me?" sort of way. Then they both went back to eating and picking at each other from across the table. Things were definitely back to normal.

Newton met Chase's gaze, wondering if he'd overstepped. Maybe Chase hadn't meant these outings as dates, but he seemed to. The indecision was frightening, and he felt a little like a teenager.

"You handled that well," Chase told him, then sipped some of his coffee. "You know, maybe you and I could go out on another date together... eventually." He winked. "Guys, would that be okay?"

Eric shrugged again. "As long as you don't do something super fun without us."

Newton tried not to laugh but didn't succeed. "Sure. Chase and I will make sure our dates are extra boring and dull to ensure that all the good stuff we do is with you." He tried to keep the sarcasm out of his voice, failing miserably. Not that it mattered; sarcasm was completely lost on his nine-year-old. Eric went back to eating as though what Newton had said was some sort of important promise that, if broken, would shake the universe to pieces.

After the snack, Newton drove home, and the kids raced inside. Eric went right to the Lego set Chase had brought, sitting at the coffee table and getting to work. Newton brought Chase something to drink and offered him a seat before checking on Rosie, who had plopped herself in the family room just off the main living room, diligently unwrapping her L.O.L. doll. Newton returned to the living room and sat next to Chase, who leaned against him slightly.

"This was a nice day," Chase said. "I had fun."

"Me too." Though Newton was a little worn out. "Eric and Rosie have so much energy, and I try to do something fun each weekend. I was thinking we could go to the zoo next Saturday." That was, if Eric didn't have another episode. It had been months since he'd had one, but that didn't mean that the next one wasn't right around the corner. The doctors had told him that with the physical changes his body was getting ready for, the POTS would become harder to manage. They also warned him that puberty was going to be hell on both of them just because of the sheer number of changes his body was going to undergo.

Eric looked up from where he was assembling his Legos.

"Are you understanding the directions?" Newton asked.

Eric held up the booklet, which was mostly pictures, to his great relief. "Reading is hard sometimes," Eric said honestly.

"We're making progress on it, though," Newton said. He didn't want Eric to think that his difficulties weren't surmountable. "He has some comprehension issues that I've been working with his teacher on. I was thinking of trying to find a tutor for some one-on-one instruction. He seems to respond much better to that kind of learning environment. The school has provided additional instruction, but they'll only go so far, and I think Eric needs a little more." He leaned forward and ruffled Eric's hair, and Eric turned to Chase.

"Do you read a lot?" Eric asked.

"All the time. I write a lot too." Chase leaned forward to speak to Eric. "I spend more time writing my arguments and briefs, documenting my cases, and making sure my arguments are sound than I do actually standing up in court." He sighed and checked his watch. "I really think I should get going. I can probably get a few more hours of work done today, and this case is turning out to be much thornier than I thought it would."

"Okay," Newton said softly, and leveraged himself up off the sofa. He walked Chase to the door. "Thank you for coming."

Chase smiled and leaned closer. "Thank you for having me. It was like I could be a kid again for a little while. I liked that." He kissed Newton gently. "I really enjoyed myself." Chase's gaze flicked to Eric, and then he kissed Newton harder, with enough passion that Newton's eyes crossed for a second.

"Ooooh," Rosie sang as she came in the room, and Chase pulled away, blushing. "Kissing."

Chase looked like he'd been caught with his hand in the cookie jar, and Newton turned away until things cooled down in his pants. "I'll call you soon."

Newton swallowed. "Yeah…." He breathed, or at least tried to. "I'll be looking forward to it." He tried to smile and not seem too goofy.

Chase left the house, closing the door, and Newton sighed, watching him as he made his way down the walk. The man was gorgeous, stunning, and try as he might, Newton didn't look away until Chase got into his car. Then Newton turned back to his daughter, who stood next to him.

"That wasn't very nice," he said gently. "Sometimes adults want a little time to themselves." It had been so long since he'd truly allowed anything for himself, and now it seemed someone might like him for him, and not because he could help the PTA raise money or spend the time to organize a bake sale for the school.

"Sorry, Daddy," Rosie said as she hugged his legs.

Newton stroked her hair and stood still for a few moments. He'd never considered himself lonely, but maybe he was. He had the kids, but that wasn't the same as having someone who was there for him.

"It's all right, honey. You go on and play. It's okay. I didn't mean to sound mad." He smiled, and Rosie seemed happier. She went back to her toys, and Newton slowly climbed the stairs to his room. He was exhausted and needed some time to himself. Not that he expected much of it with the kids up, but he lay down, putting his foot on a pillow, and closed his eyes.

The memories churned up by the flashback cascaded through his head. So many times he wished they would go away, that he could forget about them and not think of that day any longer. But they were fresh in his mind once again, like they would recede to the back of his consciousness, but only for a period of time, and then they demanded to play again and again.

The phone rang in the house, and Newton forced himself to get up.

"Dad, it's Gramma," Eric called.

Newton groaned as he got his feet under him and went back down the stairs. One of these days, he was going to have the landline service disconnected, and then she'd have to use his cell. "Hello," he said after Eric handed him the phone.

"I've been giving things a lot of thought… about you and how you're raising those kids. If you're going to be going out to see men, spending all kinds of time away while those kids are home, I'm not going to stand by and just let that happen."

"Mom, what do you think I'm going to do? Leave the kids home alone while I go out on the town until all hours? Are you crazy? I'd never do that, and you know it."

"I don't know anything, but I'm not going to allow it. Those kids need a stable home, and—"

"Now stop right there. These are my children. I adopted them, and I love them." Newton turned to where both Rosie and Eric were staring at him. He put his hand over the phone as his mother went on with her views on his parenting, not that Newton was listening. "Go on and play. It's okay."

A knock at the door drew his attention, and Eric hurried to get it. Chase stepped inside to grab his jacket, which he'd forgotten, and Newton caught his eye. He must have looked as shaken as he felt because Chase hurried over. "What's going on?"

"My mom," he whispered, and Chase nodded, going to the table and pulling out a chair. His unquestioning support surprised and warmed Newton.

"Who are you talking to?"

"A guest," he answered.

"Is it him?" she spat, venom coursing through the line. "This needs to stop. I talked to Elder Marcus, and he explained that we have a duty to protect the children we care for and not let them fall into the grip of evil. I've kept quiet for long enough because it was just you, and you put all of yourself into helping my grandchildren."

"They wouldn't be your grandchildren if I hadn't taken them in and cared for them."

She scoffed. "If you'd have gotten married and had kids like a normal person, there wouldn't have been any need for you to adopt. And that doesn't matter. I'm going to call and report you. Someone has to do something, and if it's me, so be it."

Newton practically laughed. "Who are you going to call?" He raised his eyebrows. "My boss? The people I work with, who know me and my kids and have seen me with them?" He had had more than enough of this. "Maybe you'll call the police. Be sure to ask for June Brighton. She's the officer I regularly work with on the children's protection task force. Maybe you'll talk to the officer who does my periodic background check. He'll have looked into your background as well." Newton heaved in breath as his head pounded, and he thought the walls were going to cave in. Her threatening his children was low and the worst thing she could do to him, and she knew it.

"I will do something."

"Fine. You do that. In the meantime, since you've threatened me and the kids, we will not be visiting you any time in the future. You are not to come here under any circumstances. I have a witness sitting right here with me. He has heard my end of the conversation, and he understands that I am talking to my mother, Nadine DeSantis, of Heather Avenue in Shorewood." He made sure to give all of the pertinent information.

Chase took his hand and held it, giving him strength Newton hadn't known he needed.

"You can't stop me from seeing my grandchildren," she demanded.

"Yes, I can. As their parent, I can set any rules I deem appropriate, and I just set them in front of a witness. I will also be informing their school that your ability to visit or pick the kids up from school has been revoked." Newton knew all the things he needed to do and would see to it. "Don't you ever threaten my kids or me again. I won't stand for it. Eric and Rosie are wonderful, and they deserve better than that... and so do I." He couldn't take any more of this. "Goodbye." He put the phone back in its cradle and hobbled to the table, slumping into the chair next to Chase.

"It will be all right," Chase said.

Newton wasn't so sure. Rosie and Eric loved their grandmother, and she was the only one they had. Why couldn't she see that everyone had the right to live their life the way they wanted? "I know, but the kids are the ones who will be hurt." He put his hands over his face, letting the darkness envelop him for a few seconds. Newton needed to let the anger lessen.

"Is part of this from what happened earlier? Sometimes the effects of a flashback can linger for quite a while. I know it wasn't a good conversation." Chase scooted his chair closer and took Newton into his arms, holding him.

"Was Gramma naughty?" Rosie asked as she came in from the family room, and Newton groaned. The last thing he wanted was to try to explain to the kids that their grandmother didn't accept him. In his mind, his mother was being a bigot, but he knew a lot of what she was saying was coming from one of the elders, a younger man who felt his beliefs were the only right ones. And he was determined to instill his brand of righteous indignation in his entire congregation. Newton's mother was way too susceptible to him.

"Yes. Your gramma was naughty." A simple explanation was all she needed to know. "Where's Eric?"

"Building with his Legos. I want to build too, but he said I couldn't." She stuck out her lower lip.

"Did Eric ask to play with your dolls?"

She shook her head. "He doesn't play with them right."

"Maybe he thinks you won't play with his Legos right. That was a gift to him. Let Eric enjoy them the way you did your L.O.L. doll. Okay?" It was only fair that Eric got a chance to play with his things too. Eric rarely messed with Rosie's things. He wasn't interested, and he usually shared his things with Rosie, eventually.

"Okay." Rosie left the room.

"Rosie!" Eric groused a minute later.

"You weren't playing with these!"

Newton pushed himself out of his chair to see what was going on. He arrived just in time to see Rosie tip the box of Eric's Legos on the floor. Newton was seconds from going off like a rocket.

"That wasn't very nice. Those pieces are all part of Eric's rocket ship, and he needs all of them," Chase said really gently. "Do you understand? Maybe once he's done, he'll show it to you, because it's going to be so awesome." Chase smiled, and her petulant upper lip disappeared. "You wouldn't like it if he took some of the pieces to your dolls."

Rosie nodded and began picking up the pieces and putting them back into the box. Chase helped her, and Newton sat down, taking deep breaths. The pressure seemed to be coming at him from multiple directions. He needed some quiet and maybe a little peace in order to let his head settle, but it wasn't going to, and this stuff with his mother wasn't helping.

"Eric, would you take Rosie into the family room? I think your dad needs a little silent time."

Eric nodded and gathered his things in the box. Then he took Rosie's hand and led her out of the room.

Newton put his head back, his spirit spread so thin, he felt it was going to break at any minute. Chase gripped his shoulders. Newton stiffened as Chase rubbed up and down his arms before moving upward once again.

"Did I tell you that when I was in college, I took a night course in massage and earned extra money as a masseur? It was part of how I paid for my degrees." He slipped his hands below Newton's neck, slowly massaging until Newton's head rested in his magic hands. This was what he needed. "Just let it go. Take the stress and all those things that are running through your head and let them go. I know what happened today, but just close your eyes and think of where I'm touching you." He continued working up the back of Newton's neck.

"It's difficult."

"Then just focus on my voice. Let everything else go."

Newton closed his eyes, blocking out the light, concentrating on where Chase touched him. God, he wanted to lie down and let Chase have his entire body. This was heaven. Chase's slow, gentle tugs and the heat did amazing things with his muscles. "Chase...."

"Don't move." Chase carefully laid Newton's head against the back of the sofa cushion.

Newton kept his eyes closed. The kids were playing and not fighting; his head was quiet, at least for a few seconds. He had no idea where Chase was, but at the moment, he didn't really care. He was relaxed, and the tightness in his chest was gone. Newton breathed deeply in and out as footsteps approached.

Chase's hands were back, slicked with lotion, and they started their amazing ministrations, working gently over his jaw, neck, and throat.

"Oh God." Newton breathed softly. "You don't have to do this. I'm sure you have things to do."

"They'll wait," Chase whispered, stroking his skin. "I have my work at home, and I can do it tonight. Right now, you need me more." He slipped his warm hands around the sides of Newton's neck and over his upper chest.

Newton breathed deeply, his skin heating as he wished they were alone and his shirt could magically disappear like they did in the movies sometimes. Yeah, that was it. In the movies they'd cut to the lovemaking montage, where sometimes you got a peek at the guy's incredible butt. That was what he wanted—a love montage that lasted for hours. The thought was already raising his temperature.

"You seem better."

"Yeah." His thoughts settled back where they belonged, and Newton realized his head wasn't running in flashback circles, the kids were being quiet, and he was truly relaxed. "Thank you." Newton opened his eyes and sat up straighter. Chase's hands slipped away, and Newton missed the touch almost immediately. "What did you come back for?"

"I forgot my jacket," Chase whispered, and sat down next to him on the sofa. Neither of them said much as Newton leaned against Chase, sighing softly as he tried to keep the wolves of his thoughts at bay.

"Daddy!" Rosie hurried into the room and jumped up onto the sofa next to him. "I can't get this on my doll." She pressed a small doll and an even tinier set of shoes into his hands. "I can't see it good enough."

Newton took the pieces and did his best to get the shoes onto the doll for her. She must have been happy because she hugged him, slid off the sofa, and raced away.

Soon she was back with her dolls, playing on the coffee table. Eric came in as well and showed them how far he'd come along in putting together his Lego space shuttle before setting up shop on the other end of the table.

Newton closed his eyes again, listening to the kids play and Chase breathe next to him. Chase's arm slid around his shoulders, and Newton sighed softly, letting himself sink into this fantasy of a family. The three of them had always been a family—Newton knew that and had worked very hard to build that sense between them—but now he was realizing that there had been something missing... or some*one* missing. Someone to walk the path with him. Maybe Jolene was right. He had been alone for so long, he hadn't given himself a chance to let himself have that one person to go through life with.

Honestly, Newton had never thought he would have that. Even after all this time, he'd never let his heart sprout wings. He always kept his feet firmly planted on the ground and in reality. Newton took care of the kids and built a life for the three of them. That was what was important to him: stability and what was known and what he could count on. But maybe there was more to life than that. He saw others having it, but Newton tried not to take flights of fancy. Maybe he'd been wrong. Maybe he needed to give his heart a chance to soar.

CHAPTER 4

"CHASE," MILTON said as soon as he answered his phone. "I need to see you in my office, immediately."

"All right," Chase responded, then hung up his desk phone. He gathered his papers and a copy of the Anderson file, and headed down the hall to the senior partner's office. His assistant ushered him inside and immediately closed the door.

"I've been reading your case documents, and these aren't a winning strategy." Milton set down the file.

"There's only so much I can do. Some facts are above refuting and have already been proven in court. No subsequent judge is going to take them into dispute. We know this, and I have explained that to our client. Those parts of the case are already closed, and we know that family court is not going to allow us to reopen a criminal matter. What I've done is cast doubt on the mother's competence. We have to make her the center of the case. The father has turned a corner in his life, and we are building evidence to support our case." Chase stepped closer, opening his copy of the files.

"I understand that. But you are never going to get her medical records. We can subpoena them all we want, but they are considered legally private unless she provides permission to unseal them, and she never will. Therefore, the three years of treatment could be said to be the result of our client's son's behavior." Milton had a real head for cases and arguments.

"I'm aware of that. I have a petition prepared to allow us to have a court-appointed doctor examine her and a psychiatrist to perform an evaluation. We need something that's verifiable."

Milton nodded. "But that's a huge unknown."

Chase sighed. "Yes, it is. But it's all we have. Our client can pay as much as he likes and can come into court with our entire law firm sitting behind him. But in family court, it's always what's best for the child that matters. I've studied thousands of cases, and there is no record or precedent for a judge giving potential custody of a child to anyone with this type of situation. None." He closed the file. "We never should have agreed to take this case, no matter how much money they threw at us."

Milton's eyes grew stormy, but Chase didn't back down. "The partners felt it was something we could win. And it's a chance to set a real precedent."

Chase wasn't the one who had conducted the initial interview. "The client has lied to us on multiple occasions." He pulled out the client interview sheet. "Half of this intake sheet is either an evasion or a falsehood." The unsaid portion was that the partners had been duped. But they weren't going to like hearing that. "And because of that, this is our best strategy."

Milton sat back, his eyes becoming less threatening. "I see." He folded his hands in front of him. He didn't pick up the pages again or even move much other than blinking. "You're the expert in this area. But we have to find a way to diminish the impact of their son's past."

"There is very little we can do. It's legally accepted as fact." This entire case made Chase feel as though he were walking on quicksand. The situation was hitting too close to home for his comfort. As a lawyer, he knew he would have to take cases he didn't like or agree with, but this one made his blood run cold. "I have a few ideas. I'll add them to the case documentation and discuss them with the client." There was nothing else he could do, and Chase felt that Milton was coming to understand that. Some cases weren't winnable. It was part of Chase's job to advise them about what he thought their prospects were, give advice, and then they ultimately made the choice of how to proceed.

"All right." Milton leaned forward. "You have a real sense for these kinds of cases, so I'm going to go with your instincts." That was one hell of a compliment. "I'll also speak with the other partners. You see if you can't make the clients happy and the firm look good at the same time."

"I'll do my best." Chase left the office and strode to his own, putting on his game face to look as though he wasn't upset and as though this damned case wasn't unsettling his entire world.

"William," he said as he passed his assistant's desk. "I'm going to need an hour, so don't let anyone disturb me unless the world is coming to an end." He needed a chance to think.

"You have a meeting in fifteen minutes with one of the interns. Let me see if I can reschedule that to tomorrow. That will leave much of your afternoon free. Tomorrow is going to be busy, though."

"Just reschedule the meeting for four o'clock today. That will give me what I need." Chase went into his office and closed the door, knowing William would take care of him. He could be a real bulldog.

Chase collapsed into his chair and closed his eyes. This entire case brought his own issues to the front, and he wasn't dealing with those well. His clients were trying to get custody of their grandson from their former daughter-in-law. Their son had physically abused their eight-year-old grandson. They claimed their daughter-in-law was unstable and a danger to their grandson. However, their son was scheduled to get out of jail in six months, and Chase was well aware that it was likely he would end up living with his parents. The entire case was a mess, and there was no good solution for the child. But the truth was, Chase believed that what his clients were saying about their daughter-in-law were exaggerations at best and possibly outright lies.

He reorganized his file and set it on his desk, taking a deep breath and trying not to wonder about the child involved. As much as he loved to win cases—and he truly loved it—this was only a loser. Winning in court—making the best argument and having the judge not only get it, but select it as the better one and award his clients what they had sought—was totally awesome. It was why he did this job. Lawyers were supposed to be ruthless and do everything the law would allow to benefit their clients. And normally he was more than willing and able to go that route because what he thought and felt didn't really matter. Chase could do what he needed to in order to win the case, or at least have a chance to win. This case....

He read through what he had so far. It was a train wreck, not because he hadn't done a good job, but because he found himself on the side of the argument he didn't want to be on. Chase closed the file, slamming his hand on top of it. He wished to hell he had stepped back and let someone else handle it. Hank Reynolds wouldn't have any trouble taking this case. He'd sell his mother up the river if he thought he could win. The man had no heart and no conscience. Maybe that was how Chase needed to be.

Chase pushed his chair back and tried to clear his mind, but it was damned near impossible. He reached for his phone and sent a text to Newton, receiving a call back within seconds.

"You okay?" Newton asked immediately.

"Yes. I just wanted to hear your voice. How is Eric?" Chase glanced at his phone as his line indicated he had an incoming call. William must have answered it, because the line went dark and nothing came through his email. Chase leaned back and relaxed for a few seconds.

"He's doing well. Finished the space shuttle, and it looks great. He asked me to get him another kit. I think you really started something. He sat at the table for most of the evening putting that together. I'm going to go online and see what I can find."

"There's a great Lego TIE Fighter. It has more pieces, and it's super cool." God, he wanted to get one of those for himself.

"I see. Someone has been researching Lego building sets. I wonder why?" The amusement rang in Newton's voice. "I used to love them when I was a kid." He sighed. "I bet they're still somewhere at the house." A sadness sounded in Newton's voice.

"I take it you haven't figured out a way forward."

"It isn't likely to happen. She called the department and made a report about me. The reasons she gave were laughable, but I told my boss to send a caseworker to the house tonight so they can see that everything is as it should be. That way they can't say that they're playing favorites."

"If she continues, I'll help you with a restraining order. At least it will put the system on notice that she's the one with the problem."

"I hope it doesn't come to that." Newton seemed defeated, and Chase hated it. This was really hurting him, and Chase could wring Newton's mother's neck for that. But yet he understood it. Chase had encountered dozens of reasons why people took each other to court: greed, intimidation, power, to correct injustice. The list was as long as his arm. Why would he be shocked at religious conviction? In one way it was commendable, and yet hurtful at the same time.

"So do I. But you have to protect yourself and the kids. If she's gone this fanatic, then how likely is she to listen to reason?" He hated even suggesting it. She was Newton's mother, after all. But people had been hurting one another in the name of religion for many thousands of years, so how would that change because people were supposed to be enlightened and modern?

"I'll think about it. If she continues, then the department will come down on her for making false and harassing reports."

"I really want to help."

"Just listening is helping," Newton said. "And I wish I could help you, but I know you can't even talk about it."

"Nope. But I was wondering if you'd want to have dinner? I could stop after work and get some carryout. Though I won't get out of here until seven or so." The pile of things Chase needed to do was growing, and wallowing wasn't going to get them done.

"Then stop by. I'll have fed Eric and Rosie, so if you could bring grown-up food, I'd much appreciate it." Newton paused and spoke to someone else. "I need to go. There's a crisis brewing that I need to handle. Call me when you're on your way." His tone seemed brighter, and Chase found he had something to look forward to.

"I will." He ended the call and unlocked his computer, getting to work.

CHASE KNOCKED quietly on the front door, and Eric opened it to let him in.

"Dad hurt his foot," he said, closing the door behind them.

"Are you all right?" Chase asked when he found Newton on the sofa with his foot up and an ice pack on his ankle.

"I'll be fine." Newton motioned Rosie over. "You need to go upstairs, take a bath, and get into your pajamas. Then you can come down here, and I'll say good night." He seemed drawn, and Chase had a pretty good idea that Newton was in pain but probably didn't want the kids to be upset. "Eric will take his shower after you."

"But I want—" Eric said.

Newton flashed him a look. "You've both been tired. Eric, go drink something and have the bag of chips I set out on the counter." Rosie went upstairs and Eric into the kitchen without another word. The crinkle of the potato chip bag followed by the sharp crunch of the chips made Chase smile. Newton sighed.

"Why are they being so docile?" Chase asked. It wasn't like them to be that quiet.

"I hurt my foot because I stepped on one of their toys, which they had assured me they'd picked up. Eric helped me to the sofa, and Rosie got me set up with the ice." Newton shifted himself so he sat partially up, wincing as he moved his foot. "I should have been watching where I was going and the places I put my foot, but I went down, and they both feel bad about it. Eric had a rough night last night, so he's really tired, and so is Rosie because she wakes up whenever there's activity in the house, so going to bed a little early isn't a bad thing."

He winced and waited for the pain to pass. "Are you done?" Newton asked when Eric came back into the room. "Did you get plenty to drink?"

"Yes." Eric held up the empty bottle, and Newton smiled and nodded.

"Go throw it away and then show Chase your space shuttle." Newton rested his head on the sofa.

Eric raced away, then returned seconds later to take Chase into the sunroom. He pointed to where the completed model sat on one of the shelves that ran around the entire room just below the ceiling. "Dad said I could put it up there," he said proudly.

"Did you have fun doing it?" Chase asked.

"Yeah. It was cool, and I could follow the instructions." Eric could barely sit still. "Dad said that if I'm good, he'll think about getting me another one for my birthday."

"You did a really good job." Chase figured things that required instructions and steps were good for Eric. It taught him to follow directions, and putting Legos together took time and patience. He'd talk to Newton about getting him another set.

Newton called Eric back, and Chase followed, picking up the bag of food he'd brought and taking it to the kitchen. He put the aluminum foil pans in the oven to keep them warm and went to sit near Newton as he controlled the chaos that seemed to be getting ready for bed.

Rosie came to say good night. "I'll check on you before I go to bed, I promise," Newton told her. "I can't go up the steps and come back down again."

Rosie hugged Newton and Chase before going upstairs. Eric came down in his pajamas, and they both got hugs again. Newton checked that Eric's new nighttime heart monitor was in place and that his phone was receiving the signal. Then once he was upstairs, the house grew quiet. Newton sighed, and Chase went to the kitchen, made up two plates, and brought them in.

"Oh God," Newton groaned as he took the first bite. "Did Garth make this?"

"Yes. I called and told him I needed something nice and simple that I could keep warm. He made the pesto with chicken and added just a little pepper to give it that zing." Chase took a bite, and the flavor was incredible, finishing with that hint of heat that added a level of complexity to the dish. "Are you in as much pain as I think you are?"

"Probably." Newton removed the ice and set it aside. "I'll be all right. It's just a sprain, and I'll be okay with some rest. The muscles in that ankle aren't that strong to begin with. It will feel better in a few days." He ate some more, and a little of the tension left his face, though the wrinkles around his eyes told of Newton's discomfort. "Thanks for bringing this. I really needed to see you. The last few days have been.... I should be used to handling all of this by myself by now. But this stuff with Mom is only adding another layer of stress."

"Has anything else happened?" Chase asked, then took another bite. "Sorry, we should have something to drink."

"There's Pellegrino in the fridge," Newton offered.

Chase got two cans of the blood orange soda, handed one to Newton, and then sat down again.

"No. Nothing else has happened, but the whole incident has raised hackles at work, and my boss called me in to find out what was going on. I explained it to him, but they have to investigate everything.

Of course, after they stopped by and found nothing, I hurt my ankle. It's been a crappy day."

Chase set down his plate and took Newton's hand. That simple touch warmed his heart, and as he watched, some of the stress leached out of Newton's expression.

"But it's getting better now. How was yours?"

"Equally bad, and it isn't going to get much better. I have a client meeting tomorrow afternoon that I'm dreading because they aren't going to like what I have to tell them. It's part of what I do, but clients sometimes kill the messenger." Chase picked up his plate again. "You need to eat." He motioned to Newton, who began eating the pasta once more.

"I worry."

"Of course you do. She's your mother, and this kind of break is going to be hurtful." Chase leaned closer. "At least you're dealing with it. And your mother is going to have to realize that you're the parent now. Mothers always see their kids as children, no matter how old they are."

"Yup." Newton went back to his dinner, humming lightly under his breath. "This is so good." He groaned softly, and Chase felt the sound deep inside. Damn, he wanted to hear that sound again, only maybe sometime when Newton was upstairs in his own bed, the two of them behind locked doors. Chase swallowed and leaned closer. Newton smiled and did the same, their basil-spiced lips meeting in a flurry of heat.

Newton stilled and then grinned against his lips. "I'm waiting for one of the kids to come down."

"I know exactly what you mean." Chase grinned in return, meeting a half-lidded gaze with his own. "I know we can't, but if we were alone, I'd carry you upstairs, get you comfortable, and do my best to rock your world." Chase thought for a second and snorted. "God, that sounded so cheesy. I think I need to say things in my head before I actually utter them out loud."

Newton swallowed hard. "It didn't sound cheesy to me. It's been so long since anyone was interested in me, other than as a son or parent, that what you said sounded smooth and kind of sexy."

Chase put his hand on Newton's forehead. "Nope, no fever."

Newton shook his head. "Come on. I'm a forty-two-year-old gimpy guy with two kids. I don't exactly have guys beating down my door. There's one of the ladies at work, Jolene, you might have come in contact with her."

Chase had, a number of times.

"She tried to fix me up with a friend of hers a few years ago. That was a disaster. We never actually went on the date. She set everything up and started to tell him about me. The thing was, she mentioned that I was a really great guy and that she had known me for years. Jolene is a talker."

"God, yes. Get her on the phone, and she can fill the rest of your day."

"Exactly. Well, she mentioned that I had two kids. I had adopted Rosie about six months earlier, so she was three, and he about flipped out. She never got to the part about how I used a cane. That didn't come up before he had the date canceled and was running the other way. To her credit, Jolene told him off and said that if he was that big a buttwad, she wasn't going to have anything to do with him either."

Chase nearly did a spit take with his pasta. "I'm willing to bet that Jolene's words were a lot more colorful."

Newton set his plate on the table, grinning. "Apparently she told him that if he couldn't give a guy like me a chance, then he deserved all he got at the bars and that she'd make him a regular appointment at the clap clinic. Of course, she didn't stop there." He sat back, and Chase leaned forward, waiting for the punch line. There had to be one. It was Jolene, after all, and she always had to have the last word. "I heard this part. She and I were at lunch, and we saw him parking his car in the lot. She walked up to him in his red Corvette, wagged her pinkie, and said, 'Compensate much...?' She patted the top of the car and clicked her tongue. 'I'm sorry about your penis.'"

"She didn't!"

"I swear to God. She told me that a Corvette is the ultimate compensation car, and she seemed to know what he was compensating for." Newton wiped his eyes with the back of his hand. "There are times when she will say anything."

"I take it he wasn't a very good friend."

"I guess not. She was really mad at him. Not that I could do anything about it. The guy was entitled to his feelings, and Lord knows, I don't want to go out with someone who will run for the hills when he finds out I have kids. Hiding it is only going to borrow trouble later." Newton picked up his plate and finished his helping of pasta. "That was so good."

"Garth sent dessert too. The man makes the most amazing pumpkin gingersnap tiramisu, so I asked him to put in a couple portions." Chase finished his pasta and took the plates to the kitchen. "Do you want it now or should we wait?" he asked, poking his head back into the living room.

"Don't you have more work you need to do?" Newton asked.

"Nope. I got everything done at the office, and miracle of miracles, I'm caught up. So we could watch a movie if you'd like."

"Cool." Newton pushed himself up off the sofa. "I need to go up and check on the kids. If they're awake, I'll say good night. But I want to make sure they're okay." He used the banister to lever himself up the stairs.

Chase looked through the DVD collection while Newton was gone, weeding through the Disney and animated titles for something a little more grown-up. There wasn't a whole lot there, but he found a couple of movies.

"*Guardians of the Galaxy*?" Chase asked as Newton came back down the stairs.

"That's great. I haven't watched a movie that wasn't *Mulan*, *Frozen*, or *The Lion King* in so long." Newton sat down on the sofa with a sigh. "Both kids are sound asleep." He checked his phone and then set it aside. "If Eric's heart rate starts racing or slows, I'll get an alarm on my phone." Newton sounded exhausted.

"Do you really want to watch? Maybe you should just go up to bed."

Newton shook his head. "I just need a little quiet." He stretched out on most of the sofa, put the ice on his ankle, and pulled a throw over himself. Chase got the movie in and going, turned out the lights, and sat at the end of the sofa, gently lifting Newton's legs and setting them on his lap. He made sure the ice was in place and settled in to watch the movie.

"Chris Pratt is really hot," Newton said.

"Yeah. I love the prison scene when he's in only his skivvies. The man fills out those shorts."

Chase slowly rubbed Newton's legs, and he relaxed. They got about halfway through the movie and Newton began snoring softly. Chase didn't move and just let Newton rest as he watched the rest of the film. Newton woke up at about the time that the bad guy was getting his and Star-Lord and his team saved the day.

"Do you want me to help you upstairs?" Chase asked when Newton stretched his arms over his head. His shirt rode up, giving Chase a glimpse of honey-gold skin around his belly.

"Honestly, I don't want to move," Newton said.

"How is your foot?" Chase had removed the ice to keep it from getting too cold.

"It's okay. I'm going to take some ibuprofen before I go to bed. Hopefully that will help with some of the swelling." Newton blinked a few times. "At least it was the bad one. If it had been my good foot, I probably would be in a chair while I recovered, but I'm used to babying this one." He sat up, carefully putting his feet on the floor. "You know, I can deal with the breathing issues, the flashbacks, and even the other health issues that spring up out of nowhere half the time. But not being able to walk very well really sucks. But I guess I'm lucky."

Chase didn't understand that. "Because you survived?" he guessed.

Newton leaned back, closing his eyes. "Well, yes, I suppose there is that. I did survive, when so many others didn't. There are times I wonder why I did. What did I do to make some higher power happy so they said, 'Hey, kid, you get to live through this.'" He wiped his eyes. "I know that's kind of simplistic, but it's the only explanation I have for that. But I know I'm lucky, because I should have lost my foot. It had become so incredibly infected, and gangrene was already setting in by the time I could get it looked at. The injury that set everything off wasn't that bad or that big, at least on first inspection." He swallowed and leaned back.

"You're not ready to tell me what happened."

Newton shook his head. "Any more than you're rushing in to tell me your deepest, darkest secret." He met Chase's gaze with such intensity that Chase wondered if Newton could see his soul. "And that's okay. It's not easy to share something that, like it or not, has become a part of our very essence. There are so many times that I wish I'd been somewhere else or someone else. But then I know I wouldn't be the person I am today. I'd have gone into the corporate world, and I never would have encountered Eric or Rosie. My family would look different. My entire life and everything that makes it up would be different. Even my values and outlook wouldn't be the same as they are today." Newton shifted, resting his foot on the coffee table and placing the ice pack back on his ankle. "I don't think I'd know myself if I hadn't been there."

Chase nodded. "Yes. I know that's true for me. But I'm still trying to figure out if that's a good thing or not. Maybe our lives would be better if...." He paused and blew out a shaky breath. "It takes trust to talk about all this stuff." .

Newton smiled slightly. "Yes, it does. Sharing the worst things in your life requires a lot. It's like letting someone else see my pain, but they know there's nothing they can do to take it away. I will live with what happened and its aftermath for the rest of my life. And it's likely that what happened shortened my life." Newton chewed on his lower lip, abusing it slightly. "When I considered adopting Eric, I actually asked myself if I would be around long enough to see him grow up and if that was fair to him."

Chase stood and took the DVD out of the player, unable to look at Newton because things were becoming so raw and he needed a minute to deal with it. While not going into detail, Newton had indeed shared some part of himself that was nearly overwhelming. "I never wanted to have kids. I was afraid of how I would react around them." It was hard for him to admit. "I didn't know if I could handle it." Chase put the DVD in the case and closed it, then turned off the television and the player. "I love Eric and Rosie. They almost instantly touched my heart, but they scare me too." He lowered his head, afraid to turn around. "They still do in some ways." He was being enigmatic, but his heart pounded in his chest as his past bubbled forward in his mind.

"I think you and I have talked enough for today." Newton sighed. There was something raw and chillingly close in his voice. Like his emotions were just as near to the surface as Chase's, threatening to break through in a pretty messy way.

"Let me help you up the stairs." Chase turned and guided Newton to a standing position, taking part of his weight as they made their way to the steps. It was slow going, but Chase got Newton up to his room.

Chase stood outside the door to the bedroom, glancing inside the spartanly decorated room. He turned across the hall to Eric's room, the door open, a light glowing just enough that he saw the trees and dinosaurs painted on the walls. It was the perfect boy's room, and Newton had gone to a lot of effort to make it special for him. Chase suspected Rosie's room was similar, but yet Newton's room was little more than a monk's cell. Clearly his efforts all went for the children and not himself.

"I'm okay now."

Chase stepped closer to Newton. "You're so much more than okay." He slid his hands along Newton's cheeks and around his neck, drawing him closer. The kiss was intense from the very start and only grew more heated with each passing second. Chase's head spun, and he took a wobbly step back. It took all his willpower to pull away as each cell in his body pressed him forward. He swallowed, blinking rapidly. "I think I'd better go now." He tried to catch his breath. He had to put some distance between him and Newton. "It's getting late, and…." He turned to look toward Eric's bedroom. He might have wished that things were different and that he and Newton could just fall into bed, but that wasn't possible. Newton was a father, and there were the kids' feelings and needs to consider. Besides, Chase could be patient, and he was certain that Newton was worth waiting for.

"Yeah," Newton breathed.

Chase stepped closer, whispering softly enough that only Newton could hear. "If you weren't hurting, I'd take you in there and make you want to scream loud enough to wake the dead. But the kids are right there, and you need a chance to rest." He tugged Newton into a tight hug. "But I can hold off." He locked gazes with Newton. "I have a feeling that you're going to be well worth it." He captured Newton's lips once again until Newton pressed to him. Then Chase backed away, head whirling, and lightly stroked Newton's cheek before taking the few steps to the stairs. He turned to wish Newton good night, then used the banister to steady himself as he went down.

Chase turned out the lights and made sure the door locked after him before going to his car to drive home to his empty house.

CHAPTER 5

THE FOLLOWING Friday, a file landed on his desk with a thud, and Newton lifted his gaze to where Jolene stood across from him. "I think this is one that's right up your alley. I don't have any room in my schedule, and I was hoping you'd be able to take it."

Newton didn't touch it right away. "And I'm just sitting here twiddling my thumbs," he teased with a smile. They both knew Jolene never asked for help unless she was buried ten feet under. "What is it?"

"Mother fighting for custody of her kid. Father is in jail, but will probably be getting out soon. His parents are fighting for the son because they say the mother is neglectful. I did a home visit and found a woman struggling to make ends meet, but the home was clean and she was feeding her son. The parents have more money than God and are really pressing for custody. She has custody now because the father was in jail for child abuse. He apparently has a temper."

"So when he gets out, he isn't going to live with the mother and his child, but most likely with his parents." Newton was getting a good picture of what the parents were trying to pull. Get custody of the son in their names, but the father would be the one raising—and most likely terrorizing—his son. "Of course I'll take over the file." He opened it and did a quick review. "I see the in-laws have called to report her on a number of occasions. Was there anything factual to what they were saying about her parenting skills?"

"Not that I saw. She wasn't inattentive when I was there, and as you can see, the reports are vague with no real supporting evidence. The sheer number of calls is what put her on our radar."

"Then I'll take it from here." He sighed as she sat down. "So this is a sit-down kind of visit."

"How are things going with you and your hot man?" She winked at him. "I saw him at the courthouse a few days ago. He stopped to talk for a few minutes but then had to run off to court."

"He's good, and things are going well. Chase brought me dinner when I sprained my ankle a few days ago." Newton had it in a brace, which helped a lot, but getting around was still more painful than usual. "We watched a movie, and then I was tired and the kids were in bed, so…."

She grinned. "Are you telling me you finally got some? 'Cause your sex life is about as interesting as six hundred miles of Nevada desert at twenty miles an hour. That's wonderful." She smiled, and Newton grew serious and met her gaze.

"No. He saw me upstairs, and then after a kiss that would stop time, he went home." Newton figured Chase was trying to be nice and considerate, but Newton was seconds from bursting whenever Chase was nearby.

"He went home?" She clicked her tongue. "That's interesting."

"I know. I mean, there's never going to be a time when the kids aren't around, and we can't spend our lives with the kids at the sitter or away at camp or something. I don't quite know what to do."

"Tell me about it. Kids are the world's best birth control, let me tell you. But I think what you might try is making arrangements. Get the kids in bed and close their doors. Then set up your bedroom as an enticing love nest—pillows, a great duvet. Make it inviting and sumptuous, and put a lock on your door. When you're in there, yeah, you'll need to be quiet, but it should be a haven, and Chase needs to know he's welcome there."

"Should I send him an engraved invitation?"

"Don't be a smartass. But invite him to stay and tell him what the deal is, or ask him over and have him bring a bag and then tell him what you'll make for breakfast." She wagged her eyebrows. "Not everything is perfect, and Chase certainly can't read your mind. So tell him what you want. I bet he wants the exact same thing." She winked at him. "Heck, if you were into women, I'd be interested in you."

"Thanks," Newton said, rolling his eyes. "If I were into women, you'd have ended up a man, and we still wouldn't have the right equipment, more's the pity."

Jolene snorted and stood to leave. "That's pretty good. You need to work on your snappy comebacks." She paused with her hand on the door. "I'm serious. If you're interested, then woo the guy. It really works, and guys like to be wooed just like girls do. It also helps to tell him where he stands. We all like to know that. That angsty teenager stuff really just sucks." She opened the door and stepped out of the office.

"Yeah, it does," Newton said, but she was gone before he could say anything more.

He grabbed the file and read through it more thoroughly, then made some notes on the things he had to do, including meet with the in-laws to check the veracity of their claims. He also needed to schedule another home visit with the mother and son to check on things from their end. This smelled fishy to him, and he wanted to get to the bottom of things. Based upon the sheer number of calls to child services, his supervisors were going to want a reason why the child wasn't in protective custody, but given the circumstances, Newton had cause to be suspicious, so he added his thoughts into the online file, along with his plan to investigate the claims further. That would do for today, and he'd have to get on it first thing Monday. But he had a number of cases he wanted to put to bed before the weekend, so he got on those.

"Is Mr. Chase going to come to the zoo with us?" Rosie asked as she bounded in on his bed the following morning. Rosie always woke with such energy. She was his instantly awake and happy baby.

Newton checked Eric's heart monitor app to be sure everything was okay and got his mind in gear. "I don't know." He then sent Chase a text. "He might have to work today." Newton had asked him earlier in the week, but Chase hadn't known how much he was going to do at the office.

His phone buzzed with a message. *I'm at work right now. What time are you going?*

Late morning. There's a Red Robin near there that the kids like. I was going to take them there and then go to the zoo. Newton yawned, and Rosie watched expectantly. He was about to say he didn't know when he got another message.

I have about two more hours of work here. I can come over after that. He sent a row of smiley faces.

"Is he coming?" Rosie asked, pushing her glasses higher on her nose.

"Yes. Chase is going to come." Suddenly Newton was as wide awake and excited as Rosie. "Go get dressed and then wake your brother." Rosie bounded out of the room, and Newton sent another text. *I was wondering what you'd like for breakfast tomorrow morning. I make some pretty mean morning food.* He pressed Send and held his breath.

The display remained still, no message or even the little bubbles to say Chase was writing. Newton got out of bed, determined not to watch the screen as though he were desperate. He used the bathroom, and when he returned, there was a message on his phone.

I love all things breakfast. With grinning faces this time.

Newton smiled to himself, even as his nerves kicked in, a million questions running through his head. *Will I remember what to do? God, what if he's disappointed? Has it been so long that my body has forgotten how?* Newton knew he was probably being damned silly, but he was keyed up. His body wasn't as lithe and supple as it used to be. Granted, he wasn't ready for his dotage either.

"Dad," Eric called, pulling him out of his thoughts and back into the moment. "I can't find my blue shoes."

Newton sighed. "First thing, you need to brush your teeth and clean up. Second, they're where you left them last." He pulled on a pair of light sweats and went to see what his kids were up to.

COFFEE, HE desperately needed coffee. Newton started a small pot as he put bowls, cereal, and milk on the table. He cut up some bananas for Eric and Rosie, doing his best not to inhale. He hated them with a passion, so he avoided bananas if he possibly could. But it seemed he was in the minority as far as his family was concerned.

Cartoons began playing in the other room. "Eric, turn off the television and come in here and eat." He knew his kids so well. "Rosie, stop playing in the bathroom and come down. Breakfast is ready." Yup, he had eyes in the back of his head.

The kids trooped in. "Did you put...?" Rosie started. "You did. I love bananas." She grinned at him because she knew he hated them.

"Yes. The things I do because I love you." Newton kissed the top of her head. "Now go ahead and eat your breakfast. Remember that Chase is going to come to the zoo with us and we're going to get some lunch, but not until later. So eat well." He poured milk for Rosie and then let them eat, trudging back upstairs so he could get cleaned up and dressed. Damn, he needed coffee.

By the time he was dressed and cleaned up, the kids were done, and he put the rest of the food away. Both of them had put their dishes in the sink, which was a God-ordained miracle. They were watching cartoons, so Newton took the chance to sit down in his favorite chair for a few minutes with his coffee. His ankle was getting better, but he'd put his foot brace on, and that would provide added rigidity and support if he was going to be walking through the zoo.

How long Newton relaxed, he wasn't quite sure. It was a wonderful morning, and Newton had had one hell of a week, so he closed his eyes and rested until the doorbell rang. Eric hurried by him to open it and let Chase inside.

"Can we go to the zoo now?" Rosie asked as she bounced next to the sofa.

"Yes. We can go. Turn off the television and put your toys away." He got up, using his cane to take some of the weight off his foot.

"Are you sure this is a good idea?" Chase asked. "It hasn't been that long since you hurt yourself."

"I know. But I promised the kids we'd go, and they've been looking forward to it. Since it's autumn, Eric can do more because it isn't too hot or cold, and I don't want to deny him if I can. I'll have to take it easy, and I can rent a scooter if I have to." Newton smiled. "I'm glad you're going to come with us."

"It sounds like fun. I haven't been to the zoo in years." Chase hugged him tightly as Rosie and Eric got their things.

"Do I need my monitor?" Eric asked.

"Yes. Get your bag so we can put it in the car. Then you need to put on jackets in case it gets chilly, and we can go." Getting two kids ready for a trip anywhere could be a trial, but today seemed to go well, and soon enough they were all in the car and on their way.

"How was work? Did you get done what you were hoping?" Newton asked Chase.

"Yes. Did you have a good nap?" Chase teased.

"I was just resting my eyes and waiting for you." Newton tried not to yawn. A nap, even for a few minutes, was a rare thing, and he had enjoyed it.

"I was waiting for you too," Rosie said from her car seat. "When we get there, will you lift me up so I can see everything?"

"We'll make sure everyone can see. I promise." Chase grinned, and both talked as he drove, their excitement growing.

"I wanna see the penguins," Rosie said. "And the bears and elephants."

"I want to see the snakes," Eric piped up.

Rosie ewwed and said, "I don't like the snakes."

"How about if I take you to see the birds while your dad and Eric see the snakes?" Chase offered.

"But I wanna see the birds too," Eric said.

Newton groaned. "We're all going to stick together. Rosie, you can hold my hand when we see the snakes, and Eric isn't going to take too long." He hoped that would make both of them happy. Sometimes things could get to be so complicated. "Now, there isn't going to be any fighting. We'll have fun, and there isn't to be any whining either. It's going to be a great day. Okay?"

"Yes, Daddy," Rosie answered, with Eric following along.

"They're good kids," Chase said.

"Yeah, but it's been a long week." Newton's ankle was aching, and by the time he got to the restaurant, parked, and had slid into the booth, his foot was killing him. He kept it to himself and managed to use the area next to the wall to put his foot up. That eased some of the pressure, and he sighed, opening the menu and helping the kids order.

"You look pale," Chase said.

"I'm a little tired, I guess." Newton decided what he wanted, and they all placed their orders with the server.

Their lunch was nice, and the kids ate, colored, and talked while Newton sat back and tried to make the best of what was turning out to be more difficult than he had expected. As long as he sat down, he was fine, but after lunch when he stood again, the dull ache returned. Still, he got into the car and drove them to the zoo.

Newton ended up riding the smallest, most cramped scooter he'd ever seen. It barely had enough room for his foot, but allowed him to get around so the kids could look at all the animals. Chase was so good with them, and Newton rolled along in the chair, having Eric sit occasionally, as they went ahead. It wasn't the kind of day he would've liked to have had, but he had promised to take the kids, and Newton did his best to keep his promises.

"Can you watch the polar bear with us?" Rosie asked.

Newton nodded, following her into the exhibit, where the four of them could see the bear as he played in the water. Rosie pressed her face to the glass to get a better view, and Newton sat next to Chase, leaning slightly against him.

"Maybe we should go get ice cream so you can sit, then go home. You're in a lot of pain, and don't tell me you aren't. I can tell by your face." The scooter wasn't exactly comfortable, and he was having a hard time finding a position that didn't make his foot throb.

"Okay." Newton was too tired to argue, and Chase was great at getting Eric and Rosie to agree. They left the zoo after a stop at the gift shop and to return the scooter. Chase drove, and Newton sat in the passenger seat, his leg stretched out, breathing deeply, the aching subsiding with less activity.

At the ice cream stand, Chase got the kids cones and got Newton a strawberry sundae and brought it to him. He was so grateful. Having someone take care of him was pleasant, and once he was done and the kids were back in the car, he leaned his head back, closing his eyes.

Newton had never given much thought to how nice it was having another adult around.

Chase took care of the kids and made sure they all got inside the house, then helped Newton to the sofa, got his foot on a pillow, and took off his shoe and brace. "You need to take better care of yourself." He checked Newton's foot over, his touch so gentle and caring.

Newton expected Chase to make his excuses and go on home, but Chase wandered into the other room, and soon Newton heard squeals and laughter from Rosie and giggles from Eric. Whatever they were doing, the kids seemed happy and to be having a good time.

"How about watching a movie?" Chase offered. "Your dad's foot is hurting and he did too much by going to the zoo, so we all need to be extra careful and good. Okay?"

Newton couldn't see them, but Chase's voice was bright with a touch of depth underneath.

"*Mulan*?" Rosie asked loudly, and in his mind's eye, Newton could see her jumping up and down in excitement.

"How about something else?" Chase offered.

"*Spider-Man*," Eric said. "I don't want to watch *Mulan* or *Cinderella* again. How about *Cars*?"

Rosie didn't seem to object, and both kids came into the living room. Rosie climbed onto the sofa with Newton, sitting by his legs, looking worried as her thumb made its way to her mouth a couple of times. Newton didn't scold her, because she was a big girl now, but she did pat his foot a few times and say something gentle that he didn't catch. Chase put the DVD in the player and sat down in the chair near Newton's head, reaching over and holding his hand for a few minutes.

Newton just let go. He'd been holding on to the kids, to being a parent, and in that mode for so long, he really didn't know what exactly he was feeling, but some of the tension and worry that had been part of him for so long slipped away.

"I'm thirsty," Rosie said.

"Then you and Eric get something to drink. You can have juice or milk," Newton offered, and both kids hurried away. "Thank you for not running for the hills," he said softly. "I know this is a lot more than you bargained for, and—"

Chase got up and cut him off with a kiss, sending Newton's pulse racing and his mind on a flight of fantasy that he wished wouldn't end. It all pulled to a stop when Rosie and Eric returned, and Chase started the movie. Well, everything except the hand-holding, which ended at some point in Radiator Springs when Newton fell to sleep.

When he woke, it seemed they had agreed on another movie, because *Planes* was playing. Both kids were enthralled, and Newton wondered where that had come from, since they didn't have it on DVD.

"I have Netflix, so I signed into my account. After this it's *Cars 2*." Chase set plates on the coffee table with chicken nuggets and tater tots. Both kids ate and watched, and Newton shifted to get comfortable again. Chase put ice on his foot, which was feeling somewhat better now. "I ordered something for our dinner. It will be delivered pretty soon." He smiled, and Newton's stomach rumbled at the thought of whatever delectable feast Chase had in store.

The movie ended, and Newton sat up, feeling a bit like a sloth after lying down for so long. "You both need to get ready for bed," he said, to groans, but the kids were both sluggish and tired, and went upstairs without further complaint. They had all had a busy day.

A firm knock sounded on the door. "I'll get the food," Chase said, going to answer it.

"What are you doing here?" a familiar voice demanded, and Newton groaned.

"Mother, what's going on?" He got his cane, leveraged up to his feet, and hobbled over.

She barreled her way inside. "I decided that I had to see what was happening here, and it looks like I got here just in time." Her eagle-eye glare alternated between him and Chase. "Where are the kids? Are they upstairs?"

"Keep your voice down. They're getting ready for bed."

She headed to the stairs. "I'm packing some things for them, and they're coming home with me. Elder Marcus says that sometimes we have to take matters of salvation into our own hands."

"Stop," Newton said firmly. "The kids aren't going anywhere with you, and you need to leave. This whole idea you have in your head is nuts." He pointed to the door. "You'll do no such thing." Newton's head began to ache, and his foot hurt again, heart pounding in his chest. He felt as though he was going to topple over at any second. "I don't know what's going on in your head, but it's bullshit. You have no rights here. I've met with child services, and there is no issue. Rosie and Eric are well cared for and happy." He stepped closer. "Just because you don't like that I'm gay and Elder Marcus is egging you on, doesn't mean you have any rights here. I suggest you leave now. I will have the police called, and you will be escorted off the property. If I have to, I'll get a restraining order, and if that happens, you will never see them again."

She put her hands on her hips, staring at him the way she used to when he was seven and had taken a cookie without asking. "You won't do that. Those are my grandchildren, and—"

"They're my kids, and I love them and would never do anything to hurt them. Now, as I said, you need to leave." He opened the front door. "Your religious beliefs and those of this ridiculous Elder Marcus have no place here. Just because you think something doesn't make it real or right." He stood firm, wondering to himself what had happened. This was not like the church he'd been raised in. Yes, they had very strong beliefs, but largely Jehovah's Witnesses were pacifists. They spread their word, but they were rarely as forceful and combative as this guy seemed to be. Either that or his mother was taking his messages and twisting them into whatever justification she seemed to want. "You need to think about what you're doing, Mom." Cooler heads needed to prevail somehow. This was going down a road that neither of them was going to be able to stop if they continued to escalate.

"Mrs. DeSantis, I think it's time for you to go," Chase said softly, but the anger in his eyes on Newton's behalf was reassuring.

She looked at both of them. "Next time...."

"There isn't going to be a next time, Mom. Chase will start the paperwork for a restraining order once he gets back to his office."

"On what grounds?" she demanded smugly.

"Threatening your son and trying to kidnap the children," Chase said plainly, and she paled. "That is what you have attempted to do tonight, and it's what you've threatened to do when you return. I heard it, and so did Newton." He turned. "Unfortunately, Rosie and Eric heard it as well."

Damn, Chase had the frozen glare down pat. The temperature in the room plummeted by ten degrees in seconds. Newton hoped he was never on the other end of that look. It was intimidating as hell, and his mother must have felt it too. She turned without another word and left the house.

"Daddy," Rosie said, sniffling as she came down the stairs once her grandma had left, "is she going to take us back to the orphanage?" She trembled as Newton held her.

"No. You are never going back there. I told you when I brought you home that you were going to live with me forever and ever, and I meant that." His own control wobbled as he made his way to the chair, letting Rosie climb onto his lap. "I know your gramma is mad, but that doesn't change how much I love you and Eric. She isn't going to take you away, and you don't have to see her if you don't want to." He couldn't believe he was actually saying that about his own mother. "I promise."

Eric hugged him from the other side, and Newton comforted both his kids from the hurt and fear instilled by one of the last people he should have to worry about. This was way too much, and Newton had to put a stop to it.

"But Gramma said—"

"I know what she said. But she's wrong. She can't do those things she wants, and if she tries, I'm not going to let her." Newton closed his eyes. "You two go on up to bed, and I'll be up in a second to tuck you both in."

They left, going up the stairs with none of their usual energy. Newton tamped down his anger and told Chase he'd be back, following them up the stairs.

Rosie talked for a long time before she settled enough to go to sleep. Newton checked that Eric had his heart monitor on and said good night, making sure his son was comfortable and felt safe again. Unfortunately, that wasn't going to be as easy as a simple talk.

Newton went back downstairs. Chase had gotten the food when it had arrived, and his plate was ready. They sat in front of the television. Chase had put *RED* on, and they started the movie as they ate. Newton found it difficult to get into. Not that he didn't like the movie, but his mind was elsewhere. Chase must have understood, because he paused it.

"Are the kids okay?"

Newton shook his head. "Those kids, my babies, have been through more than anyone their age should ever know, and for my own mother to come into their home… our home…." He set down his plate and reached for a tissue. "She scared them, and I doubt they are ever going to want to go see her again." He wiped his eyes and then turned away to blow his nose. "It's her own fault, but it's going to be weeks before they start to feel safe again. And I'm willing to bet on Monday that both kids are going to feel sick because they're afraid if they go to school, they won't be able to come back home." That reminded him that he was going to take them to school and revoke his mother's permission to pick them up. He should have done that already. It was clear he had to make sure that was done. "She took that away from them."

"We'll gather the information you need for the order tomorrow, and I'll draft it and give you the instructions to file it with the court. At least that should protect you."

"But isn't there a conflict of interest or something?"

"No. Because in essence you'll be doing it yourself." Chase sighed and pointed to the plate. "Your food is getting cold." He finished his dinner and took his plate to the kitchen. Then he quietly climbed the stairs and came back down a few minutes later. "They're both asleep."

Newton sighed. "That's good. I hope they stay that way." Some of the tension that had been surrounding him faded, and Newton ate the piccata that Chase had gotten. It was tangy, and the sauce was incredible, setting his tongue to dancing. He finished off the food, feeling even better now that his stomach was full.

Chase took care of the dishes, which was so kind, and when he returned, they watched the rest of the movie. Newton tried not to fall to sleep. He wanted to spend time with Chase, and he managed to make it through the movie. Then they decided it was time to go upstairs, and Newton's belly butterflies began fluttering. He needed to get his doubts under control, because he wanted this.

Chase turned out the lights and walked up the stairs with Newton, who leaned on him. "I hate that you're hurting."

"Me too." But the pain in Newton's foot quickly receded as heat and Chase's rich scent enveloped him. "It's been a long time for me." That was hard to admit.

They paused at the landing, and Chase leaned close, his lips right next to Newton's ear. "I know you aren't a virgin." His voice was so soft that Newton had to strain to hear it, but damn, he didn't want to miss a single syllable. "And virginity isn't something that grows back...."

"No. But what if I forgot…." Damn, he hadn't meant to actually say that. Newton wanted to clap a hand over his mouth. "I mean…."

Chase raised his gaze toward the top of the stairs, and Newton pressed upward. This wasn't the place for this conversation, and he was relieved when they made it to his room and Chase silently closed the door. "You aren't going to forget how to make love. You know that." He approached slowly as Newton sat on the edge of the bed, trying not to sigh with relief. He wanted this, he really did, though he couldn't stop the nerves from racing forward again and again.

"There's something I have to tell you," Newton said, patting the bed beside him. "I haven't told you much about what happened, but I'm willing to guess that you've picked up on some things."

"Yeah. You were there on 9-11, weren't you?" Chase asked.

Newton nodded. "I was there when the North and South Towers fell." He tried to keep himself together. "It was after college, and I was working at a relief agency that served the homeless. We fed them and tried to find housing and get them the help they deserved. But on that day, after the first plane hit, we knew it was going to be bad. The director asked if anyone would be willing to take the mobile kitchen down there. He said that everyone was going to be affected and that it was all-hands-on-deck time." Newton's skin began to itch and crawl as he talked about it, just like it had for days when he couldn't get the dust off him. He stilled his hands, knowing it was just a memory, but it seemed so real for a few seconds.

Chase put an arm around his shoulders, and Newton pulled away for a second, the sensation unexpected. He turned to Chase, who seemed hurt, and leaned against him.

"Sorry. When I talk about this, sometimes it's like I'm there again." Newton paused a few seconds. "Look, this isn't the time for a long, drawn-out story to try to explain my own neuroses. And I have enough of them, let me tell you."

"You're probably right," Chase said, not moving away. Instead, Chase held him for a while and then positioned him back on the bed with pillows to prop him up. Chase got Newton settled, his foot resting on a pillow, and then he sat next to him. "Now that we're comfortable, you tell me whatever you want me to know."

Newton closed his eyes, and instantly he was back there, the day bright and sunny, the sirens blaring from all directions. Without thinking, he turned his gaze skyward toward the billowing black smoke and flames coming from the Towers, and said the same prayer he had that day.

"The mobile kitchen was a converted and reinforced ambulance. I parked a block from the Towers and set up shop. The noise was indescribable, a million sounds all rushing to make themselves heard over one another. I opened the window and had granola bars, water, and was getting chicken soup and stew heated up when a sound from up above blocked out everything else. I didn't know what it was at the time, but now I know it was the South Tower collapsing. It fell on the kitchen. All I can remember of that moment is the world coming to an end and me pressing myself to the floor of the converted ambulance, hoping my death would be quick and painless." He hugged himself and tried not to let the memories and fear carry him away.

Newton opened his eyes to ground himself in the present. He was in his own room, and the screams and deafening roar were only in his head. This wasn't happening now. He breathed deeply through his mouth, and there was no grit or dust to fill his nose and throat, just regular air.

"The cab of the ambulance had been damaged, so it wasn't going anywhere unless it was towed, but the kitchen area came through intact. The North Tower fell, but it was farther away, so the impact to me was a little less."

"And you served food through all that?" Chase asked, gaping at him.

"That first day, I don't remember very much. I was on a sort of autopilot, I guess. I handed out water and granola bars because they were packaged. Somehow, I have no idea why, I thought to close the serving window at some point, or it shook closed, but that kept some of the dust out of the interior. I cleaned everything, including the stove and the rest of the interior, and on the second day, I served everything I had. People ate and went back to work on the pile. So many times I had to evacuate because of other building collapses and a million other scares and worries. I lost friends in the Towers." Tears ran down Newton's cheeks. "My freshman roommate, Carmello, worked in the

South Tower. He was on one of the floors that was hit by the plane. I only hope he didn't feel any pain."

"Was he the only person you knew?" Chase asked.

Newton shook his head, hesitating over whether he should go down that particular path. All of this was so wrapped up together in his head after all these years that it was almost impossible for him not to, but then.... He'd already gone this far down the rabbit hole, what was a little deeper?

"No. My first serious boyfriend was in the North Tower. He was above the fire. That's all I really know. His remains are some of the hundreds that are either unidentified or will never be found. Anthony and I had been going out for a month, but it had been serious and we were already talking about a future together." Newton shook his head, trying to get those thoughts to go away. He had to make them leave. This was not at all how he had envisioned this night with Chase. "I remember trying to call him on his cell, but not getting an answer. Then the dust and stuff must have worked its way into my phone, because it shorted out and never worked again."

Newton pulled out his phone and brought up a file he'd kept through a number of cell phones and various providers. Years ago, he'd saved it as an audio file, and it was on every computer, phone, and tablet he'd ever owned. Not that he listened to it all that often, but as long as that file existed, some part of what he and Anthony had, even for a short time, still existed. "When I got a replacement, I found this message waiting for me." He played the recording. The quality wasn't very good, but Anthony's voice still sounded the same, a voice reaching across years and miles of experience.

Newy, I'm up in the office and can't get down with the fire in the way. The building keeps groaning, and there is smoke coming in from the stairs and even the vents. I don't think I'm going to be able to get out, so I want to say goodbye. I love you, Newy, and all those plans we talked about, I want you to do them with someone else. You get that house you said you dreamed about, with a fence and a dog, start a family of your own, see the world, help those who need it even if they don't realize it, and find someone to dance with on the balcony of a beach house on the Gulf. I don't know how much time there is left. The smoke is getting worse and people are jumping out, falling past the windows. He coughed, and Newton turned away, burying his face in Chase's shoulder. *I do love you, Newy, and if by some miracle I do get out of this....* The recording stopped. It always ended there, and judging by the time on the tape, everything in the North Tower had ended at that exact moment.

"My God," Chase whispered, his fingers running through Newton's hair.

Newton wiped his eyes, feeling like an idiot for crying after all these years. "Lots of people got messages like that. I'm told they have a repository of them at the museum at the site." He sniffed a little and swallowed hard around the lump in his throat.

"Have you ever visited the museum and memorial in New York? It's quite moving. I've only seen it after dark, but with the water and the lights, under rows of trees, it was very beautiful."

Newton shook his head, unable to answer for a few seconds. "No. After I finished working there, I found another job. I couldn't do disaster relief, and I was lucky enough to get the job here. I haven't been back to New York since." He felt a little cowardly about that, but he knew he needed to avoid his triggers, and that site was a flashback trigger waiting to happen. "Someday I think I'd like to go, but I haven't gone yet."

Chase nodded, and the softness in his eyes was like he truly understood. "Can I ask, did you hurt your foot in the collapses?"

"No. That was my own stupidity. A few days after the disaster, there was someone else in the truck with me. The rescuers called out that they were approaching a critical time to find anyone still alive and that they needed all the help they could get. I put on a mask and a suit and offered to help." God, that was the one thing he'd do differently if he got the chance. "The pile was still burning and hot from down below. One of the things we did.... There was a ruined sporting goods store—the front was gone, and everyone needed shoes. See, it was hot enough that the soles would melt. So we took what we needed, and the searchers switched shoes. A half hour on the pile, and then they switched to a different pair to let the soles firm up again. I stayed too long on the pile. There were so many pathogens in the rubble that I got a bad infection and it ate away some of the muscle. They weren't sure I was going to live or if they were going to have to take my foot."

"So you were lucky? Or just plain stubborn as hell." The understanding in Chase's eyes told Newton that he'd made the right decision in telling him.

"Lucky, I guess. After I got out of the hospital, I went back to work in the truck for three months. I used a cane and kept my foot wrapped, and I was forbidden from going anywhere near the pile. But I was determined not to lie down on the job. My foot did heal, but it's still weak. It aches sometimes, and will be that way for the rest of my life. I have breathing issues, and I've been through treatments for lupus that thankfully is in remission right now. All of this is because of the work I did then."

"And PTSD?" Chase asked. "That's what we saw at the fun center."

"The burning popcorn scent triggered me, and I was right back there. I couldn't breathe, and the towers were coming down around me again. Same at the restaurant when we were having dinner. Something was burning, and it threatened to trigger me, so I had to step away. I used to be afraid to sleep at all because what happened would play over and over again. For a while I took sleeping pills and drank to try to forget and sleep. It didn't do me any good, and my counselor helped me realize what I was doing to myself. I can cope with it now, and the attacks are fewer and farther between. Sometimes if I know about a trigger, I can prepare for it and the effect is minimized. It's easier to deal with the known. But there will be a time when something will happen and I completely flip out. I don't know when or what exactly will cause it, but my mind will think I'm back there." Newton sighed and closed his eyes. He was so drained and tired, he'd have thought he'd run a marathon instead of just spent time talking, lying on a bed. But then, there was no way he could ever run a marathon, not if he trained for a million years.

Newton expected Chase to tuck him into bed, say good night, and most likely make his excuses and go. Chase was a nice guy, a good person, but his baggage had been a lot for him to carry around, and he really didn't expect that Chase was going to be willing to take it on.

And as expected, Chase slipped off the bed, so Newton closed his eyes to block out the sight of Chase leaving the room. The lights clicked off, and Newton started when the bed dipped.

"You should get undressed and then maybe brush your teeth and things. I need to go out to the car and get my bag. I wasn't sure what you wanted the kids to know, so I left it in the car." He leaned over the bed, and Newton risked opening his eyes just as Chase kissed him. "I'll be right back."

"Okay." Newton waited until Chase left the room before sliding off the bed.

CHAPTER 6

CHASE OPENED the bedroom door to a gorgeous sight. Newton lay on the bed in boxers and a white T-shirt, chewing his lower lip.

"I'll be right back." Chase used Newton's bathroom, getting ready for bed, and then stepped out. Newton had climbed under the covers, his chest bare, eyes a little wide with wonder. Chase smiled and walked around to the side Newton wasn't using. He lifted the covers and climbed in, then turned out the light to plunge the room into darkness.

"Chase, I...." Newton tensed next to him.

"Just relax," Chase whispered as he rolled onto his side, sliding an arm around Newton's middle. "It's been a very different kind of evening than either of us planned. So just relax and think good thoughts." He slowly caressed up and down Newton's belly. "We don't have to do anything tonight other than sleep." Newton had told him a great deal about himself and had trusted and confided in him. Chase now had some pretty big decisions to make for himself. Like Newton, he had held his own secrets deep down for a very long time, and Chase wondered if he had the guts to finally let them go, the way Newton had.

"I don't know if I can," Newton whispered. "Everything that happened is so fresh and alive in my head again. They always say that talking about things makes them better, but that's bullshit."

Chase tugged Newton a little closer, pressing his chest to his back, cradling his butt at his hips. "You can go to sleep. I'm here, and I won't let anything happen to you. I know it sounds stupid, but it's real. Just let it go and be safe. Don't hold on to what happened—release it as best you can. What stays inside grows and festers like a wound. But if you let it go, then it can heal."

That was advice he needed to take for himself. But now wasn't the time for him to share his story. Soon, though... the time was coming.

He was warm and comfortable, lying still so he didn't disturb Newton, even though he was fairly certain that Newton wasn't asleep yet. "Have you closed your eyes at all?"

"No," Newton whispered, then slowly rolled over. "I thought…. No, I should have known I wasn't going to be able to sleep."

Chase pushed back the covers. "Is there a robe?"

"On the back of the closet door," Newton answered.

Chase got it and put it on, then went as quietly as he could down the stairs and into the living room. He found what he was looking for and brought up the DVD, placed it in the player, and turned on the television.

"What is this?"

"In your collection down there, I found a copy of *The Wedding Date*." He grinned, and Newton pulled the covers over his head.

"Jolene gave that to me and told me I needed to watch it. That it was funny, and might give me a few ideas about romance and getting my butt off the sofa and into someone's arms. There are a bunch of them that she foisted on me over the years. I didn't have the heart to just throw them away, so I put them in the back of the cabinet."

Chase started the movie and got back in bed. "This is cute, and after the bathroom scene, we can turn it off, I promise." He grinned and settled in the bed, gathering Newton in his arms. Chase really hadn't cared what movie he picked as long as it was light and fluffy. He figured Newton needed something different and not serious, to have a place in his head to help banish the darkness he'd allowed to run free for a while. This one really fit the bill, and soon after the bathroom scene, where they got a glimpse of gorgeous bare man butt, Newton was asleep, and Chase used the remote to turn everything off and went to sleep himself.

"DADDY!" ROSIE stood at his side of the bed, and she gasped when Chase rolled over to blink at her.

He put his fingers to his lips. "He's still asleep, and your daddy is really tired. Is your brother up yet?" Chase blinked when he saw it was after six in the morning.

She shook her head as she put her fingers to her own lips. "Did you and Daddy have a sleepover?"

"Sort of, yes." He wondered how he was going to get her to leave the room. "It's really early. You should go back to bed for a while. Do you think you can do that?" There was always hope, but Rosie looked as bright-eyed and awake as she always did, which meant she was full of energy and ready to go.

"Okay. I'll go play with my dollies." She left the room, and Newton snickered and moaned softly before rolling over.

"You're playing possum, aren't you?" Chase asked lightly, and Newton groaned but smiled.

"How do you think I get any sleep at all? They come in here every Saturday and Sunday at godawful in the morning, so I pretend to be asleep, and they amuse themselves for a while if I'm lucky." He burrowed deeper under the covers.

"Is your foot any better?" Chase asked, hoping the quiet lasted for a while longer. His body was plenty awake, being this close to Newton, and he willed it to last. Chase didn't have any illusions that there would be time for them to be together right now, but it was nice just being close.

"Yes." Newton scooted closer. "I'm going to try to stay off it today and see if it won't improve. But Eric and Rosie often have other ideas. There are also some calls I need to make for work. I have appointments in the field tomorrow, and I want to make sure they remember that I'm coming." He sighed breathily. "The house is still quiet, and whatever you did with Rosie seemed to work."

"Daddy!" Rosie called from across the hall.

"Spoke too soon." Newton pushed back the covers and slowly got out of bed. "The day is calling. Hopefully I can get her to lie back down again, but I doubt it." He scrubbed his fingers through his hair, sending the strands into a wild configuration. Albert Einstein had nothing on Newton's morning hair.

While Newton was gone, Chase slipped out of the bed and figured he should get dressed before the kids were up and about. He grabbed his bag and headed for the bathroom, where he cleaned up and pulled on his clothes, yawning as he shaved. It was a Sunday, and he was supposed to be able to sleep in, at least for a little while. Chase suspected this was a normal thing with the kids around.

"Eric, you need to eat and get something to drink," Newton said, concern ringing in his voice as it drifted in from across the hall.

Chase heard Newton and the kids going downstairs and the refrigerator door opening as he came down as well. Chase sat on the sofa, letting Newton take care of what he needed to, barely awake and desperately craving coffee.

"You're going to be fine, but you need to get some fluids in you, and this is the best way."

"Okay...," Eric groaned, but seemed to be doing what Newton wanted.

Chase grabbed his small laptop out of his bag and logged in to the system at work, figuring he'd check his messages for a few minutes. He answered some emails and sighed as his difficult client left three more voicemails while he worked. Regardless of how much Chase told them the case was most likely futile, they were determined to go forward. Milton had just shaken his head during their last meeting and seemed willing to do what they wanted as long as they were willing to pay the billable hours. Chase put the issue out of his head for the time being and closed his laptop when Rosie plopped on the sofa next to him in her pink nightgown covered in white and yellow flowers.

"Did you sleep okay?"

"Yes. I had dreams." She went on to tell him all about the unicorn and bunnies that had played in her sleep.

"Can you draw them?" Chase asked. Rosie raced away and returned with crayons and paper, setting up a drawing shop on the coffee table. Chase closed his eyes and only opened them again when Newton sat next to him, leaning against his shoulder.

"I'm so tired," he whispered. "Eric went upstairs to get dressed. Rosie, you should too."

She looked up from her drawing and hurried away. "I'll finish that when I get back."

"She's a doll, even in the mornings." Chase picked up his laptop once again and tried to finish what he was working on.

Newton kissed him on the cheek and said he was going to go upstairs to dress, but when he got done, he'd make breakfast.

"We can do it together," Chase offered. Newton nodded and then turned. Chase watched Newton go, worrying about his foot and reminding himself to check it once he could get Newton to sit down.

Chase growled under his breath as he returned to the brief he was writing. The outline of his case was driving him crazy. He hated the arguments he was having to use because all he had to go on at the moment was the information from his clients. Basically, his case was a fishing expedition of motions and as much evidence as he could get to back them up. Still, if there was truth to what they were saying, then maybe the boy was better off with them. Chase hated cases like this, where he didn't have a clear sense of what was right. He had gone into family law because he wanted to help families, not tear them apart, and to him, this case didn't pass the smell test.

"Are you getting hungry?" Newton asked. Chase hadn't even heard him return, he'd been so far down this awful rabbit hole. He saved the document and locked his laptop, then joined Newton in the kitchen.

"What does everyone want?"

"Oatmeal with bananas," Rosie said.

"French toast," Eric said right behind her. "Or pancakes. Not oatmeal." He made a face.

"Okay. Is there something you can both agree on for me? I like eggs with stuff in it," Chase suggested.

"What kind of stuff?" Rosie asked skeptically.

Chase turned to Newton for a little help.

"Let me see," Newton said, pulling open the refrigerator door. "I have ham, and some onion, peppers, maybe some cheese."

"No onions or peppers," Rosie said, and Eric agreed. It seemed they could agree on something, so Chase got to work.

"I definitely want peppers and onions in mine," Newton said, getting out the juice.

"Sit down. I'll take care of it." Chase pulled out a chair for Newton and didn't stop fussing until he sat.

"Mr. Chase likes you," Rosie said.

Newton hugged her. "Why do you say that?"

Chase broke some eggs, listening to them talk.

"Because he held the chair for you. Gramma told me that when a boy likes you, he holds out your chair because its p'lice."

"Polite," Eric corrected. "And Gramma told me the same thing. She said it was nice. But I thought it was because she was old and the chairs were heavy."

Chase bit his lower lip to keep from laughing. Sometimes kids said the strangest things and were incredibly observant.

Chase did like Newton. He was different from anyone he'd ever met: strong, yet weak, patient with his kids, and impatient with the system he worked under, caring, and yet protective and not willing to take a bunch of bullshit. He was perfectly imperfect, and Chase liked that, because Lord knows he had enough imperfections himself.

With the eggs prepped, he chopped the ham, onions, and peppers while Newton told the kids a story about Amanda Aardvark.

"And she and her daddy, Andy Aardvark, went to get ice cream."

"Yeah, ant ice cream," Eric interjected.

"No, chocolate," Rosie countered. "Ant ice cream would be yucky." She stuck her tongue out, and Newton scolded her for doing it and then did the same to Eric for purposely upsetting his sister.

Chase got the pan hot and started the eggs for the kids, then found some bread and put it in the toaster. This entire scene seemed so domestic and normal, yet everything else in his life was so different from this. He hadn't had normal or domestic life in a long time. He got the eggs cooking and buttered the toast when it popped up. Eric was good enough to set the table, and once the eggs and toast were done, Chase served them all and took the empty place at the table.

"Is it good?" he asked Rosie. "I don't cook very often."

She smiled around a mouthful. "Good. It's good."

Eric seemed to agree, and from the way Newton was wolfing down his eggs, Chase would say they were a hit.

"Better than Daddy's."

"Yeah. He makes awful eggs," Eric chimed in.

Newton put his hand over his heart, pretending to be mortally wounded. "You can cook any time you want."

"Daddy makes good chicken nuggets," Rosie said, defending her daddy, and Newton hugged her.

"It's okay. I always consider it a win if I don't poison anyone." Newton finished his eggs, and when Chase gave him the last from the pan, Newton ate those as well. "Do you need to work?"

"No. I got done most of what I needed to yesterday and some this morning while you were upstairs." Chase checked the time, wondering if he should get out of Newton's hair. Newton had his hands full enough with Rosie and Eric and didn't need him hanging around.

A crack sounded from outside, followed by a deep rumble. Rosie practically leaped onto Newton's lap, holding him tightly.

"Rosie doesn't like storms," Eric explained. He got off his chair and ran to the front window. "Hey. Dad, it's raining really hard."

"Okay. Why don't we have a movie fun day? You two pick out a movie, and you can both watch it." Newton squeezed Rosie, who nodded but didn't seem in any hurry to let go of her daddy. "It's okay, honey. The noise is just noise."

She lifted her head, eyes meeting his. "The lightning causes the thunder. What if it comes and we all get 'lectrocuted?'"

"We're all going to be okay. I promise you. The house will take the lightning before it gets to you. So there's nothing to worry about," Chase told her. "I used to be afraid of storms too. Maybe if you're good, I'll read you a story about storms and thunder. It's called *Rip Van Winkle*. My mom used to read it to me, and I'll read it to you."

"The rain is letting up," Eric reported, "but the phone radar says more is coming."

"He's my little meteorologist," Newton explained. "Why don't you two go choose a movie together? And no fighting. I'll do the dishes." Newton got up, using his cane, and winced.

Chase helped him sit back down and loaded the dishwasher. Then he got Newton in the living room with his shoes off and foot up. He looked over his foot, which was a little red, but nothing alarming as far as Chase could tell. The swelling had gone down at least.

"I REALLY should go home," Chase said after lunch, at least three movies, and enough popcorn that he swore it was coming out his ears.

Rosie and Eric put in another movie, and Newton saw him to the door after he'd made sure he had everything in his bag.

"I had a great time."

"I know it wasn't what you had expected, and I'm sorry for that. It...." Newton was getting off on an explanatory jag that wasn't necessary, so Chase kissed him, tugging the man closer.

"I had a great time just as things were. There's no rush for the other stuff. It will happen when the time is right." Chase kissed him again. "The kids are wonderful, you're amazing, and you all made me feel like I was part of a real family again." He tried to keep the roughness out of his voice, but it was definitely time for him to go. Chase could really get used to all of this, and that was the danger. "I'll talk to you this week." He smiled and left the house, dodging puddles on his way to his car.

HIS GOOD mood lasted until he got home, and then the doubts kicked in. Chase paced the house for a long while, trying to allay his fears, but they wouldn't abate. He had to do something. He hunted up his phone and called the one person he thought could help. He only hoped she was available.

"Hi, Mom," he said when she answered. Chase had half expected to just be leaving a message.

"What's going on? Tough case? You sound awful." Hattie Matthews was never one to mince words. There were multiple voices in the background.

"I have a case that I feel like I'm on the wrong side of." Maybe that was part of what was bothering him, but it wasn't all of it.

"Give me a minute," she said as Chase was about to tell her that they could talk later. "I'm at a fund-raiser thrown by Costas's firm, and they are as interesting as a drippy faucet." The last part was whispered as the background noise dropped away. "All right, that's better. Now what about this case?"

"I don't really want to talk about it other than to say that if I win, I could be putting a kid back in the path of his abuser." The thought turned his stomach.

"I see," she said, then grew quiet. He could tell she was waiting for more. "You've had difficult cases before, and you always handle them. So, what's different this time?"

Chase sighed. "I'm seeing someone, and he's really special and I like him a lot. The man has guts in spades. He's with child services, and he fights for kids and families like a tiger." Now that he'd started, it was best to plow ahead. "He has two kids, Eric and Rosie. Eric has health issues, and I had to help Newton take him to the hospital once. Rosie has vision issues and wears glasses. I swear she has me wrapped around her little finger already."

"Ahhh... I understand." He knew she would.

"Yeah." It was his greatest fear, the one he didn't want to give a name to. "What do I do?" His hand shook a little. "What if I turn out... like *him*." He spat the pronoun like it was an unspeakable curse word.

"Aww, honey." He could almost imagine her in the room with him when she used that tone, comforting him and telling him that everything was going to be all right. "You are your own person, and you make your own decisions. The fact that you asked the question and are worried about that happening means it's very unlikely to."

"But...," he protested. It was part of what he had feared for years.

"There are no buts about it. You worry about being on the wrong side of cases with children. Just be yourself and don't worry about what happened. You aren't him, and you never will be." If she were with him, he had no doubt that she'd be hugging him right now. "Honey, I have to go back. I'm getting the evil eye from one of the other wives. But just be happy and try to let the rest go." She hung up, and Chase put his phone away, feeling a little better and hoping she was right.

MILTON MET Chase in his office on his way back from one of his Monday morning meetings. He went inside and closed the door. "Where are we with the Anderson case?"

"I have all the motions prepared, and I'm going to file them with the court when I'm there tomorrow. I thought I would hand deliver them to the clerk so there are no mix-ups. Then we'll have to see how the judge rules. I have made them as tight and compelling as I can." He did his best not to let his own feelings about this entire matter show on his face.

Milton sat down but didn't get comfortable. "We're lawyers, and there are times that we have to take cases and sides that we don't like or agree with. It's part of the job. But sometimes there are cases that we're just not able to take. If you had your own shingle, you could pick and choose the cases you wanted. And that's what a lot of lawyers do. In a firm like this, the partners are the ones who make those decisions, and that can be frustrating."

Chase wasn't sure where Milton was going with this, but he waited.

"I know this case isn't one that you're really comfortable with."

Chase nodded. That was true. "There are personal reasons. But I'm a good attorney, and I will do my best for our clients."

Milton didn't react. "I have to ask. Is there any sort of conflict of interest?"

"No. It's nothing like that."

"Good. Family law is tough. Before you joined the firm and went into this area—willingly, I might add—we had eight attorneys who did this job, and each left after two years. Family law weighed on them pretty heavily. We see people at their absolute worst, and I'm not ashamed to tell you that I would rather try a dozen capital murder cases than handle just one of the cases you do." Milton stood. "Just make this case come out positively in some way or another. Do whatever you need to. We are all impressed, and I want to hold this case up to the other partners as the one to say that you deserve to be made partner because you threaded the needle like a pro." He left Chase's office, closing the door.

Chase blew out the breath he'd been holding. Yes, if he made good, he would be a partner in the firm, but his job and reputation hung in the balance of one of the most awful, mean-spirited cases he had seen in his career. He had his strategy, and he wasn't going to back down. Still, he needed to review everything with his clients.

"William," he said. "Can you confirm with the Andersons that they will be in this afternoon? I need to go over our case with them before I file the paperwork."

"I already did. They will be here at two, and I have the conference room booked." William seemed so cheerful. "Is there anything else you needed?"

"Well...." Chase hesitated. "No, I'm fine. Thank you." He hung up, and within seconds William knocked on the door and peered into the office.

"What's going on?" William asked. "You hesitate when something is wrong and it has nothing to do with a case." He plopped himself into one of the chairs. "You only get this twitterpated when you're interested in someone or you've decided they're getting too close and you want to pull away." He glared. "You aren't going to dump that guy with the kids, are you?"

Chase shook his head. "No. I'm conflicted about the Anderson case, and it's spilling over into other parts of my life."

William gaped at him. "You never have case bleed-over. This must be pretty bad." He leaned forward. "I will say, these people give me the creeps every time I have to call them. Just talking on the phone with her makes me glad I was never into women, because this lady would freeze off anyone's balls." He shivered. "I know we don't have to like these people, but really."

"Yeah." It wasn't the people, but the situation itself that bothered Chase. "Sometimes we end up on the wrong side of an argument."

William nodded. "So this is a crisis of faith."

"I wouldn't say that."

"I would. You've always put your faith and trust in the legal system. Two lawyers arguing and battling it out in front of a judge. It's what you love, more than anyone else in this office. You revel in it, and you still think that justice prevails. And now you're worried that it won't, because even if you win this case, you'll feel that maybe you lost. How do you know that your clients aren't right and that they aren't...?" William rolled his eyes. "Okay, I get your point. I wouldn't wish that woman on anyone. But you do your job the same as the rest of us."

"Yeah, I know. But it's hitting too close to home." Chase swallowed. "I know the grandparents are paying the bill, but in a way, we all work for the little boy in this case. It's what's best for the children that we all have to take into consideration." And the thought that, if Chase did his job really well, he could be putting this particular child back in the path of the man who hurt him scared the crap out of him. "Still, I'll be okay." He checked his clock on the computer. "I need to prepare for this meeting and get some other work done."

William stood to leave.

"Thanks for listening." He could always count on William's unique perspective to help set him right. He had hired him as an assistant, but got a confidant and a friend in the process, and he often wondered what he'd do without him.

Chase continued working and ate at his desk in order to try to keep on top of everything. He managed to stay current and to prepare for his meeting with the Andersons. William sent a message just before two to say that they had arrived, and Chase asked William to sit in and take notes for him.

"Good afternoon," Chase said as he came into the conference room. He shook hands with both of them. "Would you like some coffee?"

They both declined.

William got him a cup, and Chase took a seat, opening his files. "I wanted to do a final review of the affidavit and the motions we are requesting. I have them typed and ready to go. I need both of you to read them over and let me know if there are any changes. If there aren't, you each need to sign your affidavit at the bottom, attesting to their truthfulness and completeness." He slid each their copy of the forms he was set to present to the court. Once they were done, he signed the motion.

"Will we need to testify?" Mrs. Anderson asked.

"Most likely. I doubt these motions will be granted without testimony. Your daughter-in-law's attorney is going to fight them, and that means he or she will want to question you." Chase hadn't heard if she had an attorney, but privately he hoped she did. Still, there was nothing to battle until he filed the motions, and then things would really begin to happen.

Chase waited until they had read them, verified that there were no changes, and William passed them each a pen.

"Why do we have to sign? You're the attorney," Mr. Anderson challenged.

"Because while I'm the lawyer, you are the ones making the claim, and they need your affidavit for that, and this is part of your testimony. I'm not making these accusations—you are. I'm only here to ensure that everything is done within the law." Chase met his gaze. "If there is anything that isn't truthful or accurate, you need to speak up now. Otherwise this will become part of the court records, and you will be held accountable for their truthfulness."

"This is what we told you," Mr. Anderson said.

"Yes, but do you see all of the things you describe in here?"

Mrs. Anderson nodded, and her husband did as well. Then he picked up the pen and signed the documents with a flourish. She did the same.

"Okay. I will submit these to the court tomorrow in person, and then we'll wait for a hearing date. You need to understand that what you're trying to do is a long shot. The court is not going to take a child from his mother without compelling evidence that he is in danger or being mistreated."

"I know she doesn't feed him very much. Every time we see him, he's starving." Mrs. Anderson patted her eyes with a tissue, but Chase wasn't buying that. He'd seen enough crocodile tears to know them pretty well. He always wondered at people's motivation. It was part of his job, and he was convinced that theirs was to punish the mother.

"You are also aware that your son's actions will be brought into any hearing we have," Chase said.

"Part of your job is to get that suppressed."

Chase loved this portion of any case. "I can't have court records removed. As far as the courts are concerned, the abuse and harm your grandson received at the hands of your son is a fact, pure and simple. He was convicted, and the same fact that he is set to be released in six months is also something that the courts will look at."

"But he served his time and…."

Chase shook his head. He had been over this with them more than once, and up until now, they hadn't seemed to be listening. "This is family court, so the fact that your grandson was abused is relevant. They will not put him in a situation where he can be exposed to his abuser again. If you do get custody of your grandson, I expect the courts will rule that he is not to have any contact with his father at all. Are you prepared for that?" He knew damned well they weren't. These people were under some delusion that their son still had rights as far as his son went. That was no longer true with his conviction. Children were to be protected from their abusers. "I'm going to need to know what you plan to do. If your son is going to live with you, this entire case is a nonstarter. The court is unlikely to take you seriously."

"But he's our son...," Mrs. Anderson whispered in the first real show of emotion that Chase had seen.

"As far as the court is concerned, your son is primarily your grandson's abuser. As I've told you, they will view everything from your grandson's perspective and what's best for him." Chase hoped he was getting through to them. "You need to think about what you're doing and all of the ramifications before I make any filing. The court will not look favorably on you if you change your tune midstream." He stood. "You also need to understand that if you lose—and our chances of prevailing are not good, I'll be honest here—it is likely that your daughter-in-law will not allow you to see your grandson any longer. Ever." He altered his gaze between both of them. "These sorts of things are not something most people can come back from." He sat down once again to seem softer. "Maybe you should consider if being a part of his life and being able to help him isn't a better road to take." Chase closed his file, stood back up, and left the conference room, letting that idea hang in the air. William stayed behind to walk them out, and Chase went back to his office, waiting to speak with William and get any messages.

Chase knew very well how to make an exit, and he hoped he had planted a seed that they would at least think over. This case had the potential to get very ugly, very fast.

"They didn't know quite what hit them," William said, once they were safely back in Chase's office. "Do you think it will make a difference?"

"No. They're hellbent on getting what they want and hurting their daughter-in-law instead of helping her." Chase sat down. "It's funny, but in situations like this, the mother takes as much heat as the abuser. 'Why didn't she see it? Why didn't she do more to stop it?' Abusers go to great lengths sometimes to try to hide what they're doing. That kid's mother isn't to blame for what her husband did. But it's easier for people like the Andersons to blame her than to place the cause of everything at their son's feet. She should have been more supportive, or she should have done something to make their precious little boy happier… or some such shit." Chase realized he had gotten on his soapbox and grew quiet.

"I see," William said knowingly, and that bothered Chase. He and William worked well together and he was a great person, but Chase didn't want him or anyone at the office knowing his personal business. "I'll go ahead and type up the notes from the meeting and add them to the file." William left the office, and Chase did his best to feel less exposed before he had his next meeting in half an hour.

His phone vibrated on his desk and he smiled at the message from Newton. *Dinner?*

Chase responded. *Yes.* His fingers paused over the keys. *I have something we need to talk about.* He pressed Send on the second part of the message before he could stop himself. *It's nothing bad, but I need to tell you some stuff.* He pressed Send again, his heart racing, but it was too late to go back now. He had put it out into the ether, and he needed to follow through. It was more than time that he told Newton of his past. Newton had trusted him with his worst days, and Chase should be able to extend the same trust in return.

You have me a little worried. Are you okay? Newton sent in return. *We can talk if you need to.*

Chase smiled. That was Newton, always thinking of others. *I'm doing okay. It's been a challenging day, but I'm going forward. How is your foot? Is it feeling better?* He was still worried with the amount of pain Newton continued to have.

It's better. I'm getting around as well as can be expected. He ended the message with a smiley face. *What do you want to do for dinner?*

Chase started to answer as Newton began typing another comment.

Jolene's daughter is one of Rosie's friends. She's having a birthday party on Saturday, and she invited Eric as well. He'll come home after the party, but Rosie is going to stay the night. So…. He sent a winky emoticon, and Chase smiled. *Maybe we can try again?*

Sounds good. I'll pack a bag. Now, that was well worth taking a chance on. *As for dinner, how about if I stop and get some fried chicken and bring it over? That sounds really good to me, and the two of us can talk once the kids are in bed.* It was best to get this over with and clear the air.

Sounds great. Bring some extra because Eric loves it, and even if I feed him dinner, he'll be hungry. His appetite has really been kicking in lately. Part of it is the medication.

Chase smiled. *I'll bring plenty.* He checked the time and messaged that he had to go. Then he got down to preparing for his next meeting. Now that he'd made a decision, he felt better about opening up. It wasn't like he was worried Newton wouldn't understand or would reject him. It was just that Chase had put these memories into their own box years earlier and liked to keep them there, but for some reason, they were surfacing a lot more right now, and he needed to deal with them.

CHASE RANG the bell, and Rosie opened the door with a big grin on her bespectacled face, with Newton coming up behind her.

"Daddy said you were coming and bringing some chicken." She stepped back. "I like chickens."

"Are you hungry?" Chase was suddenly worried that he might not have brought enough.

"Yes. Daddy said that it was his dinner, but that we could have a piece if we were good." She turned toward the inside of the house. "Daddy, were we good enough to have chicken?" she yelled at nearly the top of her lungs.

"You were, up until this moment when you yelled my ears off," Newton said as he closed the door behind them, leaning on his cane, a bright smile on his face. "Go on upstairs and wash your hands. You've been playing with Play-Doh, and it's everywhere." He might have sounded slightly frazzled, but he didn't look it for a second. Newton looked good, really good, in his navy polo and shorts.

"Can I have chicken too?" Eric asked.

"Go get plates, and if Chase brought enough, you can have some. Remember that you and Rosie already had your dinner."

Eric walked to the dining area, saying something about starving to death, and put plates on the table, as well as silverware and glasses. Chase set down the container of chicken and a bag with coleslaw and fruit salad in it. He pulled everything out of the bag while Newton got drinks, and they all sat down to eat.

Rosie had a chicken leg and was done, asking to leave the table to play with her dolls. Eric ate nearly as much as Chase did and then got up from the table as well, leaving him and Newton alone.

"This is good." Newton had enjoyed his chicken thigh, but loved the coleslaw, eating a great deal of it.

"It's from a little mom-and-pop place near the house. They only do a take-out business. He makes the chicken, and she does the rest. I'm not sure which is better." Chase got a helping of the coleslaw from the container. "I love this stuff. She told me once that instead of using vinegar, she uses dill pickle juice in it. That's apparently how she gets the dill flavor, and she uses the pickles as a garnish or in one of her other salads. She's really pretty amazing."

Newton chuckled. "Tell me, is there anyone in the food industry that you don't know?" His eyes twinkled.

"I like good food, and I don't get a chance to cook very often. I work late almost every night. So places that offer good, homestyle food are worth their weight in gold. I don't eat at Garth's all the time. The food is too rich. It's delicious, but I like other things. So I've made friends with the folks who help feed me." Chase finished his chicken thigh and his salads before sitting back, full and content.

"Guys, it's almost time for you to go to bed. Finish up what you're doing and put things away." Both heads turned toward him from the other room. "You can watch a video for half an hour and then go upstairs." Newton took care of his dishes and went to check on the kids.

Chase cleared away the rest and sat at the table once again. He wondered how he could put what he wanted to say into words. As a lawyer, he made his living with words. He was good at them—they were his friends, but not right now.

A video started in the other room, and Newton joined him. "Do you want to talk now, or wait?" he said gently.

"It's probably best if I get it over with. See, I know you'll understand and won't judge me or anything. It's why I feel I can tell you this." Chase took a deep breath. "I don't quite know how to start. I don't remember everything, and some of what I'm going to say was supplied by my mother." He sighed and tried to put what he remembered into something cohesive.

"As far back as I remember, I was scared of my father. That's the overriding emotion I have when it comes to him. He used to hit and spank me. Dad had little patience, and I never remember playing with him. Mom said he drank, but I don't remember that. But he was my dad, and I did what he said." Chase's throat closed up. "But what I remember most is the day that I told Mom what Dad was doing to me. I'd been afraid for weeks. I wasn't sleeping at night because I was afraid that if I did, Dad would come in to get me." Chase sighed and closed his eyes to shut himself off, but opened them again as the memories came flooding back. "My father used to come into my room at night, and that was when he—" It was so hard to say the rest, and he pushed away the fear that came rushing back, even after all this time. "I do remember falling asleep in school and falling out of my desk chair. All the kids laughed at me. They didn't understand what was happening and why I never talked to anyone." He blew out a deep breath.

"Did your mom believe you?" Newton asked.

"Yes. She did. And I thank God for that every day, because if she hadn't, I would never have been able to get away from him. She called the police and she took me to the hospital, where they looked me over. I remember them needing to see my butt." Chase sniffed. "Some things about that time will stay with me forever. The fear and uncertainty." His hand shook a little. "I know they were trying to help me, but I was so scared that Dad was going to come back and hurt me again." Chase was eternally grateful that Newton didn't ask him to go into great detail about what his dad had done.

"Yes. That's a very common reaction with kids who have said something." Newton took his hand. "I see things like this way too often."

"I bet you do. I guess I was lucky. Mom stood by me, Dad was arrested, and she fought and fought until he went to jail. They didn't have me testify because there was enough other evidence. Mom filed for divorce before he was convicted, and testified herself. I never visited him or saw him again after that. He was eventually killed in prison by one of the other inmates." Chase took a slightly shaky breath. "I know all of this is why I went into family law, because I wanted to help kids like me." And that was why he hated the case he had so very much. Everything inside him screamed that he was on the wrong side of this argument. Putting a child back into the path of his abuser was a recipe for major unhappiness.

"I guess I have to ask, why didn't you go into another area? You could have distanced yourself from the memories and trauma. A lot of people would have. They would have gotten as far away from the hurt as possible." Newton squeezed his hand.

"I know, and there are times I wish I had." Lord, Chase had nearly gone to pieces with his first case. But he reminded himself time and time again that he was doing good and hopefully helping kids like himself. "Sometimes I wonder what's real and what isn't. I mean, I think I remember things, but then I'm not sure if I really did. It was a long time ago."

"Those memories stay and linger and then make an appearance when we least expect it."

"That's true. I dream about my dad sometimes and wonder what made him be that way. When I told my mom I was gay, she asked me if it was because of what my dad had done to me." Chase shook his head. "I suppose it was natural for her to wonder."

"Yeah. Your mom probably spent many years wondering if every decision you made and even the person you turned out to be was because of what your father did to you."

Chase nodded. "Mom remarried when I was in high school, and her second husband, Costas, is a great man. He's an executive, and his career took them to New York. They have one of those beautiful apartments on the Upper East Side, and Mom is happy. She deserves to be happy."

"But what about you?" Newton asked, still holding his hand, and Chase didn't want him to release it. The connection with him seemed precious and something he didn't want to be without. "Are you happy?"

Chase shrugged a little. "I didn't give any of the stuff with my dad much thought for a very long time. I knew I was gay when I was thirteen, but didn't tell anyone, except Mom. I didn't really come out until college, but that doesn't matter too much. I was working hard then and still am."

"Do you think that the things with your dad affected the way you view relationships?" Newton asked. "I know it happened a long time ago, but our attitudes and feelings about how we view other people are often set in early childhood." He shook his head, smiling weirdly. "Now I'm sounding like one of those people who thinks they understand everything about everyone. You're an adult, and yeah, what happens when we're a kid affects us, but you have the choice to be the person you want."

"I know. It's just that I have this case, and it's getting to me." Chase paused, choosing his words carefully. "I feel like I'm on the wrong side. How I feel about my clients usually doesn't matter. Whether I like them or not is immaterial, but I really hate these people. My inner child, the part of me that was hurt, is telling me to run. But I can't." That was as close as he dared come to anything about his client.

"I know you can't say any more, and that's perfectly fine. I have a case as well... a new client, and I visited them today. It's a difficult situation. A child and his mother—" Newton stopped as Rosie ran into the room.

"The TV went off." She bounced. "Eric can't fix it, and I wanna watch the rest of the show."

"Okay. I'll come look at it." Newton levered himself up and went into the living room. He seemed to be walking better, which was a relief to Chase, but he figured that if he got the chance, he'd massage Newton's leg to see if he could make him more comfortable.

Chase took the time to put the few dishes they used in the dishwasher and threw away the trash. The TV started a few seconds later, and Chase joined the rest of the family for an episode of *Duck Tales*. It seemed that was what the kids could agree on.

"I wanted *Mulan*," Rosie said as she crawled onto the sofa and then plopped herself into his lap. "Eric says if he has to watch that movie one more time, his brains will leak out his ears." She looked up at him through her glasses, her big eyes shining. "He shouldn't do that. Eric can't afford to lose any brains."

"Hey!" Eric said.

Chase turned to Newton, trying desperately to hold in the laughter. These people, this family, were just what he needed to lift his spirits.

IT TOOK Newton a while to get the kids to bed, and Chase wondered if he should stay or simply go home. Newton had things he needed to do, and Chase knew there was work waiting for him, but frankly, he didn't want to leave. This home was comfortable, warm, and welcoming. The ghost of what he'd opened up to Newton about seemed more distant now. It had happened years earlier, and for the most part, the memories had faded, but today they had come back with more clarity than they had in a long time.

Maybe one never truly got over the shit that happened as kids. Maybe it was all a matter of learning to deal with it. Lord knew he couldn't change anything about it.

Chase spent some time alone with his thoughts, and started slightly when Newton sat down on the other end of the sofa, putting his legs across Chase's lap. "Do they ache?" Chase asked, pushing up Newton's pant leg and gently rubbing his weaker ankle and calf.

"A little. It's really much better, but the right is hurting from compensating more for the left." Newton sighed as Chase continued his slow massage. "Can I ask you something? How were things between you and your mom after everything happened?"

"Mom was a tiger. Apparently my father wanted to see me, and I heard her on the phone with him the one time she agreed to take his call. Her words were that he'd see me over her dead body and through a line of SWAT officers. I don't think he ever called again." Chase stilled his hands. "I do think my mom worried about me a lot. She used to ask me if I was all right for no reason, and she watched me all the time. I know she thought that part of me was broken. For a while I felt broken and was afraid the kids at school would find out what happened. But no one ever said anything. They didn't even tease me about my dad being in jail. I think either the teachers or the principal scared them, because there was never a word or a hint of anything. Maybe it was my mother they were afraid of."

"It sounds like you were believed and had support. It's terrible when things like this happen to anyone, especially a kid, but you'd be surprised by the number of kids who come forward and aren't taken seriously, even by the other parent." Newton lowered his legs to the floor. "I see it a lot. They aren't deemed truthful until something happens that forces the issue, and by then the abuser has had free rein for years." Newton sat back. "Do you want to talk about this some more?"

"I'd rather not. I mean, I told you what happened, but I don't want you to feel sorry for me and look at me any differently." That was what he needed more than anything.

"I won't. As I tell some of the families, they need to stick together and help each other. It's the only way to get through it. Your mom did that." Newton smiled. "Now, how about we talk about something more pleasant." He actually put his head back and began to laugh. "I'm not sure what it means that you and I have shared the very worst situations in our lives. I never talk about what happened during the aftermath of 9-11, and I'm pretty sure you don't talk about what happened to you."

"No." Chase leaned closer and touched his lips to Newton's. "I trust you."

Newton shook his head. "Me too. And I don't trust anyone easily. Not even the kids, with certain things. They don't know what happened to me, and I won't tell them until they're a lot older." He sighed. "But I got through it. We both still deal with the aftermath, but it's the hardships that make us who we are. You became a family law attorney, and I became a social worker, each because of our past." Newton gently stroked his legs.

Chase didn't move as heat built between them. This wasn't the heat of passion, but the gentle warmth of companionship and caring that had been missing from Chase's life for many years. He knew it was by his own actions. "I have a history of backing away from any relationship that gets too serious, I know that. There have been times when I've wondered why. I know none of the guys I've gone out with are my father…."

"Yeah, but have you trusted any of them enough to tell what happened to you?" Newton asked, and Chase shook his head. "Maybe that's what's been missing. If you're going to have a relationship with someone, you need to trust them enough to tell what happened to you."

"Yeah. But I knew some of these guys for a lot longer than I've known you, and I never…." Chase paused. "I was never comfortable saying anything before. I always felt like they'd judge me or look at me like I was broken." He closed his eyes, a weight had lifting off his shoulders, one he hadn't known he'd been carrying because it had been with him for so long.

He put an arm around Newton's shoulders and found a show on television that they watched without saying much. He'd never realized until tonight how nice it was to have someone to not do much with.

By THE end of the week, Chase was even more exhausted than usual. The Andersons, as he'd predicted, decided to push ahead with what they wanted, regardless of what reason and prudence dictated. He was still waiting for notification about a hearing, but expected it would be in a few weeks. He also managed to wrap up a number of other cases, so while he was tired, he was satisfied, and left the office with everything tied up with a bow, which was extremely unusual.

"Have a big weekend planned?" Hank asked as he passed his work area, a smarmy smile stuck on his lips. Word had gotten around the entire office that the partners were looking to present a single offer, and Hank, it seemed, was determined he was going to get it. "Little early?"

"It's Friday and I have my work done for the week." Chase didn't need to go into how late he worked the rest of the week, long after Hanky Panky had gone home. "How is the Carson case coming along?" It was a disaster in the making. A real train wreck that Hank had lobbied for the firm to take. There was little good that could come out of it, and Hank was walking a tightrope to keep the mud from splattering all over him.

"How is Anderson coming?" Hank retorted.

"Pretty well, actually. The clients have decided how they want to go forward, and I covered the firm's rear end, so regardless of the outcome, we'll come out of it looking okay." He patted the doorframe, turned, and headed to the elevator.

As he waited, Milton approached and stood next to him, not speaking until the doors to the car slid closed. "I heard about your little stunt with the Andersons." He raised his eyebrows, and Chase nodded but said nothing. "Good work."

"It didn't do much."

"Other than cover all of our butts. They are on notice that this is all on them, and that's what we needed. Now just get some sort of favorable outcome so we don't look like ambulance-chasing fools, and we'll all be good."

Chase turned to Milton. "There isn't a good outcome in this case. Not as far as I can see. If we win, then their grandson loses, and if we lose, then...." He left it hanging, because he'd yet to actually meet the mother. He hoped that would happen soon, so he could assess her for himself. "I'm not getting personally involved... but there has to be some sort of justice and stability for that little boy. As far as I'm concerned, everyone else can go to hell and stay there."

The elevator doors slid open and Chase said good night and headed for his car.

"MR. CHASE!" Rosie said with delight when she opened the door the following afternoon.

"What's going on?"

"Eric isn't feeling good," she told him, and Chase dropped his bag and closed the door. "Daddy is upstairs with him." He took Rosie's hand and let her lead him to Eric's room, where Newton spoke softly to Eric.

Chase waited until he came out of the room. "Is he okay?"

Newton bit his lip and lowered his gaze to Rosie. "Can you go downstairs and play with your dolls? Chase and I will be right down." He smiled, and Rosie hurried away, buying what Chase was pretty sure was an act. "I don't know. Because of the POTS, when he gets sick, it messes with his heart rate and he dehydrates fast. He hasn't been throwing up, so that's a good sign, but I always worry." Newton kept his voice low. "I'm hoping this is just because he overdid it and needs to rest. I have his heart monitor on him, and I set the alerts."

Chase poked his head into the bedroom. "You doing okay, buddy?" he asked without coming too close.

"Yes. I'm tired, and my legs hurt," Eric said, sounding miserable.

"I have compression sleeves on his legs, and I'm hoping that once we get the blood that pooled in his legs flowing, he'll feel better."

"Do you want me to sit with him?" Chase asked.

Newton shook his head. "It's best if he goes to sleep. I know that. But I'm afraid his heart rate will spike. Sometimes it's like a roller coaster."

"It hurts, Dad," Eric said, and Newton hurried into the room. "My legs." He closed his eyes, and Chase easily read the pain on his face. No one should have to go through that, and certainly not at his age. "Dad," Eric said, holding Newton's hand. Chase was about to ask if they wanted him to drive them all to the hospital when Eric's expression relaxed and he took a deep breath. "Oh, it's better now." He seemed drained, and sweat beaded on his forehead, but even Newton seemed more relaxed.

"Let's give it a little more time and maybe you'll feel a lot better." Newton stroked Eric's forehead and leaned forward to kiss it. "I'll be downstairs for a little while, but I'll come back up to check on you. I promise." He stood and left the room, his steps heavier than usual.

"How are you? Is your foot okay?" Chase noticed how he was favoring it more than usual right now.

"It's fine. The swelling is pretty much gone. I've been up and down these stairs so much today, though. Sometimes I wish I'd bought a house on a single level. But when I saw this house, it felt like home. I had Eric at the time and thought this would be a great place to raise him."

"What's with his legs?" Chase asked as they slowly made their way down the stairs.

"The blood pools in them sometimes, and when it does, they get hot and they ache. In the afternoon we try to have him sit with them up for a little while. It helps keep the blood flowing, but today he was so active, and then he felt bad. He's been resting for a while, and it finally started to flow again. It hurts when that happens sometimes." Newton wiped his eyes. "I can take a lot of pain, but I can't take it when he or Rosie is hurting."

They reached the bottom of the stairs, and Chase pulled Newton into a hug, holding him while he shook in his arms. "I wish I could tell you that everything is going to be all right." He held him and closed his eyes, letting Newton draw on some of his strength.

"Daddy!" Rosie called.

Chase released him, allowing Newton to go see what was going on. Chase went into the kitchen to make a pot of coffee. It looked like they were both going to need it.

ERIC CAME down an hour later and spent much of the afternoon on the sofa. Newton said he seemed better, but Chase knew it wasn't normal for a nine-year-old to fall asleep in the afternoon. Still, Newton said that it was usual for Eric after he had one of these episodes, so they watched him, and Newton kept checking the heart monitor. Eric's appetite seemed unaffected, which Chase took as a very good sign, and Eric and Rosie played that evening.

"He seemed much better," Chase said after Newton put both kids to bed.

"His legs are normal, and his heart rate is good and has been for a couple hours. I made sure he drank the liquid IV, so hopefully he'll be okay for the night." Newton sat on the sofa. "I have to take Rosie to the eye doctor next week. They'll want to change her prescription, I'm sure. She'll see an ophthalmologist this time because he wants to assess her condition." He sighed.

"Her sight has been improving, right?"

"Yes. But I don't know how much more they can do and how long it will last. The doctor told me that there's a good chance that as she gets older, her condition will deteriorate."

"You can't worry about what might come. She's doing well and she's happy now. That's what matters." Newton seemed to make everyone around him happy. He had certainly made Chase much happier over the past few weeks.

"I wish I could stop worrying sometimes, but I can't. I want her to have everything she wants and to have the best life she can."

"And she will, because you're her daddy." Chase leaned closer, and Newton kissed him. Chase didn't really want to talk about the kids right now, or cases, or traffic, or anything other than the fact that he and Newton had a few quiet minutes to themselves and that was what mattered at the moment.

"I'm exhausted," Newton confided.

"Then maybe we should lock the doors, turn out the lights, and go upstairs. Do you think the kids are asleep?"

"Yes. I'll check on them if you want to close up down here. Then I'll meet you in the bedroom." Newton kissed him once again and climbed the stairs.

Chase took care of things, followed him up a few minutes later, and took the dim trail of light into the master bedroom. He closed the door and used the single candle in the corner to guide him to the bed. Newton had already shed his shirt and pants, lying on the bedding in only a pair of black briefs. Damn, the man—his man—looked good. Chase paused at the thought that Newton was his man. He liked that feeling, and didn't take his gaze off Newton while he toed off his shoes and tugged his polo shirt up over his head.

"Wow," Newton whispered.

Chase dropped his pants and climbed onto the bed. He gently straddled Newton, careful of how much weight he put on him, and kissed him.

"I'm not going to break."

"But—"

Newton tugged him down, capturing him in an iron grip. "I don't want any buts...." He slid his hands down Chase's back and into his boxers, grabbing his cheeks. "Except this one."

He would have laughed at Newton's cheesiness, but those hands felt damn good, and Chase stroked over Newton's chest. It seemed what he'd thought about for weeks and come close to a couple of times was finally going to happen. Newton, at least for a few hours, was going to belong to him. His to care for and pamper, his to caress and hold, his to love on. Now that was exciting.

Chase slipped Newton's briefs down his hips and off his legs, getting the full-on effect of Newton in all his uncovered glory. He was stunning, lithe and sleek, with perky nipples that Chase circled his lips around, drawing out little whimpers of pleasure that seemed to echo off the walls of the room.

"We have to be quiet," Newton cautioned.

"Look who's talking. You're the one making all those lovely sounds." Chase smiled. "And don't you dare stop. The kids are asleep, and I want to feel, taste, and hear you." He'd had enough of words, and after kissing Newton breathless, he slipped down the bed, tracing every ridge of Newton's belly, sucking a trail that led to his long, slender cock. Chase didn't hesitate for a second, sliding his lips around the head and then down the length.

"Oh my God," Newton breathed as Chase took more and more of him, loving the way Newton vibrated beneath him. "And I was nervous that...." He groaned again, and Chase slid his tongue around the shaft. Newton sighed and gasped, the sounds building one on top of the other.

Chase was in no hurry and determined to draw out Newton's pleasure for as long as possible. He wanted Newton to experience as much happiness as he could, so he slowed his ministrations, letting the head of Newton's cock slide across his tongue.

"It's been so long. I think I forgot...."

Chase smiled and let Newton slip from between his lips. He surged upward to take possession of Newton's mouth, crushing their lips together in a bruising kiss, his own control waning. Chase wanted more, and when Newton tugged them close, their cocks sliding along each other, Chase closed his eyes, the pleasure almost too much to bear. This was amazingly warm and growing more so by the second.

Newton held him tighter, his hips thrusting upward. Chase didn't want this to stop, and groaned softly as Newton sucked at his shoulder, whimpering and then stilling as heat spread between them, the sensation sending him over the edge, and he added his own heat to Newton's.

Chase hated to move, and Newton held him tightly, both of them enveloped in a bubble of contentment and pleasure that went on and on.

"Let me get something to clean us up," Chase whispered, and reluctantly got out of the bed. He returned with a warm cloth and towel, washing up their mess before blowing out the candle and getting back into bed.

"We should put something on in case one of the kids calls for me in the night."

Chase retrieved their underwear, and they put them on before cuddling close under the covers. Newton drew closer, putting an arm around his middle. Chase held him in return and easily slipped off to sleep.

HE WOKE hours later, the room still dark, but Chase took a second to remember where he was. He looked around, and Newton kicked him under the covers, hard. He then rolled around and whimpered in his sleep. Chase touched his shoulder, and Newton bolted upright in bed.

"Oh God...." He turned and covered his face, then lay back down.

"Are you okay?"

"Yeah, it was just a dream."

"From what happened back then?" Chase asked quietly. "Do you want to talk about it?"

"No." Newton breathed heavily. "I need to check on Eric." He climbed out of bed and left the room, using his cane. Chase watched where he'd gone and waited for him to return. "Eric is fine." He seemed relieved as he got back under the covers. "I had a dream that I couldn't wake him up, and I was trying to carry him out to the car and couldn't make it. My damned leg wouldn't work, and I knew he was going to die because of me." Newton shook like a leaf, and Chase held him, hoping it would pass and he'd settle down as the dream memories faded.

"You know that isn't going to happen. You've taken care of him for years, and you will until he's out on his own." Chase wished he could make this all go away.

"Yeah. But sometimes the nightmares and the flashbacks are so real." Newton lifted his gaze. "It's hard to describe. Like the other day with the burned popcorn—for a few seconds, I was there. I could hear it, smell it. Hell, I could even see the entire world coming apart around me. It was real for me."

"I know. It happens to me sometimes. I'm that kid again, afraid, scared, and there is nothing I can do about it." Chase sighed softly, knowing the helplessness that washed over him every time he had a flashback. "What do you want me to do when they happen?"

"Just what you are," Newton answered, but Chase wasn't sure that Newton understood his question.

"I mean, what do you want me to do when you have a flashback? You pretty much brought yourself out of it the other day, but it will happen again, and I want to be able to help."

"Just be there, I guess. Sometimes if they're bad, they just need to play out. I can get lost in the flashback… and it takes some time for me to find my way out. I haven't had one of those in a few years, but then I know it's waiting for me. Something I have no idea about will trigger it." Newton leaned against him, and Chase guided Newton back down onto the bed.

"Go back to sleep if you can. I'm here, and I'll watch over you." Yeah, it sounded corny, but Chase meant it, and Newton closed his eyes.

Chase waited, and soon enough Newton's breathing evened out and he began snoring softly. Chase climbed out of the bed to get a drink of water and returned when a soft cry reached his ears.

"Daddy."

Chase got the robe out of the closet and quietly left the room. "Hey, Rosie. It's me. Your daddy is sleeping. What's wrong, sweetheart?" He sat on the edge of her bed, feeling her forehead. She was a little warm, but didn't seem feverish.

"I can't sleep." She rubbed her eyes.

"How about I get you a glass of water, and then I'll read you a story." Chase got the water, and Rosie showed him the book she wanted him to read. He turned on the little bedside light and pulled the robe closed, waiting while Rosie got comfortable.

Chase got two pages into the story and Rosie was asleep. He read another page just to be sure, then turned out the light, lifting his gaze to the doorway, where Newton stood, leaning against the frame. He smiled, and Chase got up, put the book aside, and left the room, letting Rosie sleep.

"I was trying to let you rest," Chase said once he and Newton were behind a closed door. "I didn't mean to overstep."

"You didn't. She seemed happy to let you read her the story." Newton sat on the edge of the bed. "When she first came to me, she was so shy and quiet, and she rarely spoke at all. At first I thought that maybe she didn't have much of a vocabulary, but she proved me wrong after a few days. She was one scared little girl. But once she opened up and figured out that I was going to love her no matter what, she changed." Newton held out his hands. "This is going to sound dumb, but what I remember most is the first time I knew she was being naughty."

"Why?" That seemed strange.

"It was because she knew I'd love her no matter what and she was just being herself. She knew I wasn't going to send her away." Newton sighed. "She and I had a talk about acting naughty, and then

I went to my bedroom and cried for happiness. She was part of my family. Of course, after that, she and Eric fought like any brother and sister. I knew my little family was complete. And that Rosie had me wrapped around her little finger."

Chase climbed under the covers, wondering about that last statement. Was there room for him in this family, or was he simply someone passing through Newton's life? Chase knew that part of the answer to that question was his, but the rest was up to Newton. He rolled onto his side, facing Newton, tugging him closer, and closed his eyes. Chase didn't have to have all of the answers. In this case and with this relationship, there was little in his control, and he needed to roll with what happened, or it would be like he was fighting the wind.

CHAPTER 7

"PLEASE TELL me what's been happening," Newton said to Marcia, who sat on the sofa, with her son, Joshua, playing on the floor a few feet away. He seemed to watch his mother almost constantly and refused to be out of the room from her. Jolene had come with Newton, and she managed to get Joshua to go to the kitchen with her for a few minutes. Once he was gone, Marcia answered his question.

"Joshua is scared to death that his father is going to come back. He's behind in school and doesn't want to go at all. He's afraid of the principal, who is big and tall, like his father." Marcia seemed to be holding up pretty well, which Newton thought was good. She was going to need all her strength.

"I see." Newton reached into his bag and pulled out the file. "Your ex-husband's parents have made a number of complaints, and I'm here to look into them." It was pretty easy for him to see that some of what was said was totally made up. The house was spotless, and Jolene had said that on her unannounced visits, there had been toys about, but the tiny apartment, which had definitely seen better days, had been clean.

"I'm sure. My in-laws think that because I can't afford brie, or the fancy food they stuff themselves with, that I'm not providing for Joshie. I get food stamps, and I've had issues. But I see my doctor regularly, and I take my meds each and every day. I qualified for subsidized housing, and I was lucky enough to get it. And I went to a legal aid, and they are helping me apply for disability, because I want to be able to work but can't."

That was all consistent with the information Newton had. "So why all the complaints? In their calls they have said that you aren't stable and ignore Joshua a lot of the time." That didn't seem to be the case to him.

"I don't ignore him, but some of my meds are pretty strong." She stood and opened a drawer in one of the side tables. "This is a list of all the things I take. I keep them in the cabinet in the bathroom. I was told I should lock them up, so I did. That way Joshie can't get them." She handed him the paper and sat back down. "There are times when things get really overwhelming, and my mother-in-law loves to push my buttons. Have you met her?"

"No," Newton said, hoping he never had to.

"Now they have decided that they are going to take me to court." Her hand shook as she handed Newton an envelope from the table. "They want custody of Joshie and want me to submit to a bunch of evaluations. I already have a doctor that I work with, and now I'm supposed to meet with someone from the state. They don't know anything. I've seen my doctor, the same one, since I had Joshie."

Newton made notes and nodded. He didn't see anything to lead him to believe that these charges were true. "Can I take a look around?" He wanted to be thorough, because it was likely that the judge was going to request a review of the home, and that was going to fall on Newton's shoulders.

"Yes. We don't have a lot, but Joshie has some toys and I always feed him." She turned away. "I'd make sure he got something to eat if I had to go without myself."

Joshie ran into the living room and climbed into Marcia's lap.

Newton looked in the bedrooms, which were as clean as the rest of the home. Joshie's bed wasn't made and there were a few toys on the floor, but nothing seemed unusual. The bathroom was old... as in, *old* old, and had seen better times, but it smelled of Pine-Sol and was cramped, but clean. Everything had been childproofed. Newton didn't see any evidence of neglect or a lack of care at all. He went to the back of the apartment and looked down from the second floor out into the yard.

"Is that a pool?" he asked. God, that could be a real hazard if Joshua could easily get to it.

"Yes. The owner lives downstairs, and he has the aboveground pool. There is an emergency escape through the backyard. But other than that, we don't have access."

"Great. Do you keep the back door locked?"

"Yes. It's high enough that he can't get to it, but I can unlock it fast if we need to get out."

Newton went through his list of questions and then the report on the benefits she was getting. "It looks to me like they didn't add Joshua to your file." He sat at the table, pulled his small laptop out of his bag, and booted it up. He tethered the connection to his phone's data so he could check. "Let me add him...." He hummed a few seconds, and sure enough.... "That will increase your food help by two hundred a month. It should start next month, so watch for it on your card."

She gasped. "I have been fighting for that for weeks now. They kept telling me that I didn't qualify." The expression of complete relief was one Newton never got tired of. This was why he did his job.

"You definitely do, based on everything here. When I get back, I'll follow up the trail of your case and make sure it's put to rights." He shook his head. This sort of laziness really pissed him off. "I've already requested an updated benefits letter to be sent to you."

"What about all this?" she asked, holding up the letters from the court. "I don't know what to do."

"Talk to the people at legal aid and see if they can help you. I will talk to some people I know and I'll try to see if I can find a lawyer to help you." It wasn't his job, but these people were way out of line as far as he could tell. Maybe Chase could help. "Is there a date to appear? If so, make sure you're there no matter what. I'll be sure to file my report and see to it that the court receives a copy." He jotted down the case numbers from the top of the letter so he could reference them. "I'll also make sure you get a copy. Do you have an email address?"

"Just Gmail, and I have to access it at the library."

"Give it to me. I'll make sure it's mailed and sent there too. Print it out and have it when you go to court. That should help bolster your case. I'll also be willing to testify, and so will Jolene." He turned to meet Jolene's gaze, and she nodded.

Marcia gave him the email address, and Newton hoped he could help her. If nothing else, he could be there to represent what he saw, which would go a long way toward refuting some of what was being leveled at her. Under normal circumstances, if his department found the kinds of things that Marcia was being accused of, they would take custody of her son right away. But as far as he could tell, there was no basis for doing that at all.

"What else do I do?"

"Is there any family? Your parents? Will they support you in this?" Newton asked.

Marcia shook her head. "I don't speak to them very much. I burned a lot of bridges before I had Joshie, and it's very hard to reconnect with them." She held her son in front of her.

"If I could make a suggestion. Call them and explain what's going on and what you need." Newton had seen things like this so many times in his career. "Tell them who is accusing you and that they're lying. Sometimes adversity will bring you back together. They must want to see their grandson." Who wouldn't want to be part of that little boy's life? He was adorable, with a smile that could disarm the Russians. "Also talk to friends to see if they will stand up for you. What you're going to need to do is paint a picture of how life is in your home, and they can help do that." Newton stood. "I'll see what I can do to help. I promise." He ruffled Joshua's hair and said goodbye to Marcia before leaving the apartment.

"Those reports are the biggest bullshit job I've ever seen," Jolene said. "There is nothing there to indicate anything like abuse or neglect. And it was bone clean. You can't fake that kind of thing. I looked in the refrigerator, and there was food. Not a lot, but it wasn't empty, and there were leftovers and small containers. You don't fake stuff like that."

"No. I don't see anything either." Newton shook his head and got in the passenger side of Jolene's car. "Thank God I'm done for the day." He sighed.

"I'll take you right back to the office, and you can head home. The kids will be getting off the bus soon."

"Yeah. I can write up the report on the visit tonight and get it sent out." He leaned back, closing his eyes. "I have some other things to do that I can finish once the kids are in bed." He turned to Jolene. "Thanks for coming with me on this one. It looks like the more eyes on this case, the better."

"I did dump you in the middle of this." She frowned. "Do you really think you can help her? Will that gorgeous hunk of a lawyer you're seeing be able to help?"

Newton shrugged. "He can't take the case. He's got a full plate right now. But I'm hoping he'll point me in the right direction." He felt a little guilty continually going to Chase every time he needed some help. Newton had spent years standing on his own two feet, and almost as soon as he met Chase, he'd been able to lean on him. What was he going to do if that shoulder was no longer there?

"Newton, remember that we're there to help, but we can't be the ones to do everything for each client." She pulled to a stop. "It's more than any of us can handle. All we can do is try to present the truth in cases like this. It's what the court and the department expect of us. We aren't a legal referral service."

Newton nodded. "I know that. But I've been on her side of things." The fallout from 9-11 had been overwhelming, and aid and help had been slow in coming. He'd had health issues, coping issues, wasn't sleeping, was in constant pain, sometimes unable to breathe, and he hadn't known where to turn. The government and existing programs were overextended, and specific programs for first responders and survivors like him hadn't gotten up and running yet. He hadn't known where to go for help and nearly lost his life because of it. So he knew how Marcia felt to a degree. The wolves were at the door, and she was trying to fend them off. Newton's wolves looked different from Marcia's, but that didn't mean they were any less frightening.

"You know my mother tried to make accusations against me in a play to take my kids. That's exactly what Marcia is going through. I had the wherewithal and resources to fight her. Marcia doesn't. She's relying on us to help her… and I'll do my best to try." He felt so very strongly about that.

"Have you heard anything from the dragon lady?" Jolene grinned.

"She has called and I talked to her briefly, but only to make sure she wasn't dying or something. I have no interest in any of her self-justified delusions." He had kids to protect, and Newton would do that, from the entire world if necessary. "I have everything set for a restraining order, thanks to Chase, and we'll file it if she tries anything else. I don't want to cause trouble that can't be easily undone."

They pulled into the lot, and Newton thanked Jolene and took his bag right to his car. He waved, got in, and drove to the school, figuring he had enough time to pick the kids up.

Newton snagged a parking spot right in front and was able to pick up Rosie and Eric just as they came out. They climbed into the car, chattering happily the entire time about their day. Newton smiled, half listening.

"Did you feel good all day?" Newton asked Eric.

"Yes." Eric sounded so put-upon. "Mr. Fielding had story time, and we sat on the floor. I put my feet out like you told me to do, and my legs feel good. Can I go over to Brian's house tonight? His mom sent a note with him to school." Eric passed over an extremely rumpled piece of paper. "And Mr. Fielding sent a note home with everyone." It seemed both pieces of paper were stuck together.

"You can call Brian when you get home as long as you promise to behave and to call if you start feeling bad." Newton turned onto their street and slowed, seeing his mother's car parked in front of the house, along with another.

"Gramma's here," Rosie announced.

"Stay here," Newton cautioned both of them, his defenses rising by the second. "Eric, look after your sister, and both of you stay in the car." Newton sent Chase a quick text saying that his mother had paid a surprise visit, then got out, locking the car after him.

His mother got out of her car, and another man stepped out of an old blue Camry.

"What are you doing, Mom?" Newton asked.

"This is Elder Marcus, and he suggested that the two of us try to come see you about raising your children the proper way."

"Yes, I think—" Marcus extended his hand, but Newton ignored it, turning away from him.

"Mother, I have things that we need to do. Eric is going to spend some time with a friend. Rosie and I are going to bake some cookies." He ignored Marcus altogether. His ultimate problem was with his mother, and he needed to deal with it there. "If you had called, I could have saved both of you the trouble."

"You know how I feel, and the elder agrees with me. It isn't healthy for you to raise those children with a parade of men traipsing through your house." Her tone was so haughty, it grated on his spine like nails on a chalkboard.

"How you feel, Mother, both of you, is of little concern in this instance." Now he turned to the elder. "I have no idea what sort of person you are, but pushing your nose into my family's business has cost my mother dearly. She is not going to see her grandchildren again. A restraining order will be filed with the court tomorrow, and then she will be arrested if she comes within five hundred feet of us or our home." Newton suddenly felt light-headed, and he took a step back. Now was not the time to have a flashback. He forced his mind and attention to remain where it was. "Now, both of you leave. This is 2019, not 1959. Your assumptions are insulting, and your beliefs and methods extremely outdated. And quite frankly, you are both ridiculous. Those are my children, and I love them more than life. I will protect them from narrow-mindedness, bigotry, and hypocrisy as much as I am able. In other words, I will protect them from the likes of you." Anger welled inside him. "Now go." He turned and went back to his car, about to pull open the door to get him and the kids away for a while when Chase's car came to a stop behind him. Newton had never been so relieved to see anyone in his life, especially with the way Chase raced up to him.

"Are you okay?"

"I told them to leave," Newton said, looking back to where the elder and his mother still stood. They were talking, and his mother's shoulders slumped. When she caught his gaze, her eyes shone with tears. He knew she was probably crying, and Newton was tempted to try to work things out with her. She was his mother, after all. "Should I…?"

"Nothing is going to change today," Chase said softly. "She isn't going to back down or change her mind as long as she has reinforcements with her. No matter how wrong her ideas, she thinks she's right, and she'll cloak herself in righteous indignation because of this elder."

Newton knew Chase was right, but it still hurt. After his ordeal and injury, his mother had been there beside him the entire way, and it left a cavern inside him to see how much she'd changed because of this pastor. Newton knew in his heart that if Elder Marcus had been a much more understanding and typical minister, his mother's behavior would be different.

"You're right." He stayed where he was as the two of them finally got in their cars. The elder pulled away, speeding past them, glaring as he did, as though he could make the fires of hell burn out of his eyes. His mother left as well, and only then did Newton get the kids out of the car and take them inside.

"Thank you for coming," Newton said once Rosie was settled and Brian's mom was on her way to pick up Eric. "I know you have to go back to work, but I was wondering if you have a minute?" He motioned into the kitchen and put on a pot of coffee, then took a seat. "I have a client, and I know you can't help her, but I was wondering if you knew someone else? Her ex-in-laws are making trouble for her. They have made dozens of unsubstantiated calls to Social Services, and now they are taking her to court. She needs someone to help her, and it's out of my area of expertise." He poured them two mugs and brought one to Chase, sliding it across the table.

Chase took the mug without drinking. "What's her last name?" he asked, suspicion filling his tone.

"Anderson," Newton answered. "Marcia Anderson. I did an inspection today, and—"

Chase checked his watch and stood. "I'm sorry, but I need to get right back to the office." He turned to leave the room. "I can't help this time. I'm afraid you're going to have to look elsewhere." He strode toward the front and left the house, closing the door behind him.

Newton was a little surprised, but figured Chase had a meeting he needed to get back to, so he finished his coffee, took care of the dishes, and saw Eric off to his friends. Then he went in to check on Rosie to see if she wanted to bake cookies, but she was happily engaged in playing with her dolls, so he got out his laptop, made himself comfortable on the sofa, and got to work.

"WHERE'S MR. Chase?" Rosie asked as she climbed onto the sofa to sit next to him. "If he wants to come over, you can kiss if you want and I won't look." She covered her eyes as she giggled.

It had been two days, and Newton hadn't heard anything from him. That wasn't necessarily unusual, although they did text regularly, but even that had stopped. Newton sent a message about having dinner tomorrow.

I have to work really late. The caseload is really heavy right now. Maybe we can talk this weekend.

Okay, Newton responded and didn't receive anything more. It was puzzling to him, and Newton wondered if he'd done something wrong. Maybe all the honesty and the fact that Newton had the kids was too much for Chase after all, and he was pulling away. Newton could understand that he and his family were probably a little much for a lot of people, but he thought he deserved to be told what was happening.

"Are you okay, Daddy?" Rosie asked. "You look like you could use a hug." She climbed into his lap and put her arms around his neck, giving him a big hug. "Is that better?"

"Yes, sweetheart. I feel much better." He forced a smile and hugged her again. Maybe he was making way too much of this, but Chase was always responsive, and if he couldn't talk, he'd tease and send happy faces through text. This was about as cold as the North Pole. Newton probably should have expected it. Loneliness and loss trailed around the edges of his heart, but he continually pushed them away. He had things he needed to do, and the kids needed him. That was where his mind should be, not running in circles over things he could do nothing about.

That worked while he was busy. Dinner, baths, bedtimes, stories—all of it kept him occupied until the house was quiet. Then he sat alone on the sofa, wondering again.

Newton sent Chase another message to tell him good night, and this time there was no response. Something was wrong, and Newton wondered what it was. His first instinct was to call Chase and get him to talk to him. But Newton had his pride like anyone else. Besides, maybe something had happened and that was why he wasn't hearing from him. That thought got him worried, and his parental streak kicked in. Newton sent another message. *Tell me what's going on. Are you okay?* He held the phone, watching the screen, hoping for a response. He didn't get one for almost half an hour, and then his phone rang. Newton could almost hear the hesitancy in the ring as he answered.

"I'm fine, Newton. There's nothing wrong. I just need—"

"I'm not one of your clients, Chase, and I don't appreciate the distant, lawyer voice. If you aren't happy or this is too much with me and the kids, just say so. You don't need to give me the silent treatment. I think I deserve to know what's going on, and if you don't want to be part of our lives, that's okay, but the kids deserve better than silence." Damn, Newton wasn't above using them as a little leverage.

"Newton…." Chase's tone had softened. "I don't know how to handle this."

"Okay…," Newton said softly. That told him plenty. "At least I can deal with that, and when the kids ask where you are, I can say that you have other things to do and that you're still a friend, but we aren't going to see you much anymore." Eric and Rosie would forget about Chase eventually, and they would all move on. It sounded so easy in Newton's head, but his heart ached at the thought.

"It isn't that," Chase answered quickly. "The case you asked me to help with is my case." He seemed almost pleading. "I've been talking about these people—not specifically, but in general terms— and now I find that we're on opposite sides. I could have a potential conflict of interest, and then our different perspectives of the case could have its own complications. I've told you things about my case and how I feel. I was talking to my boyfriend, and now I could have been talking with a witness for the other side." He began breathing heavily.

"This isn't a criminal trial. This is family court. You know how things work as well as I do. The judge asks most of the questions and directs where things go. But I don't know what to tell you." In a way Newton was relieved as hell. "But I have met Marcia exactly one time for a few hours. My report will be presented, and I might have to answer questions about it. But that's all."

"You were asking me about an attorney for her?"

"Yes, because she needs one." Newton took a deep breath. "Jolene can take things from here, and I'll switch some cases with her so I can step back." That seemed like an easy solution to him. "I have some flexibility in my work, and we look out for each other."

He finally allowed himself to relax. "You aren't dumping me?" he asked tentatively. God, the worry that Chase was leaving had hurt bone-deep, no matter how much he might have tried to play it down in his head.

Chase laughed. "I panicked a little. This is the first real, serious... serious relationship I've had, and I don't want to walk away from it, but for years all I've had is my career, and now this case—"

"I know. With those despicable people...."

"Yeah. It could have ruined everything, and I didn't know what to do about it, so I pulled back to what was safe." Chase sounded tired and worn-out, like he'd been through a wringer of his own. "And if I had only talked to you, we could have come up with a solution days ago."

Newton shook his head, even though he was sitting in an empty room. "Nothing can ruin anything... if we don't let it." The answer was as simple as that. "It all comes down to what you want."

"Sometimes...," Chase said, and suddenly Newton needed to see him.

"Are you home?"

"I was just going to go to my house. I had so much to do, and... my head went in circles all day."

Newton imagined Chase sitting out in front of his house in the car. He didn't know why, but thought that was where Chase was.

"I wanted to go home, and after everything and then talking to you, my car sort of made its way over here." There was a slight sniff in his voice. "I really just needed to come home and...."

Newton got up, went to the window, and parted the curtains, and sure enough, Chase's car *was* parked out front, with him sitting inside, the overhead light on. The line went quiet, and Newton set the phone on the table and slowly walked over to unlock the door. Chase came inside and immediately took Newton into his arms, embracing him in a strong hug.

Chase shook a little in Newton's embrace. "I wanted to go home, and when I did, the damned car took me here. I didn't think about it, just let it take me. All I had to do was hear your voice, and it brought me here like a siren song." Chase kissed him hard and deep, and Newton let himself go right into it, drawn to Chase's heat. But he wasn't going to let kisses and all the hotness surrounding him get him off track. He and Chase had some talking to do, and the man wasn't going to get out of it.

Newton parted his lips as Chase's tongue pressed for entrance. Chase cradled Newton's head, making his scalp tingle wherever Chase touched him.

Okay, so maybe they could talk a little later.

Newton leaned into the kiss, letting it take him away, giving himself over to it as his body reacted. Damn, he wanted this, and instinct and need were seconds from taking over. Newton pulled back, letting go of Chase, inhaling deeply to try to calm the raging desire that threatened to take him.

"We need to talk," he whispered. He managed to take a few unsteady steps toward the sofa, then lowered his body to the cushions.

Chase sat beside him, turned slightly. "I know I should have just talked to you. But this damned case is driving me crazy. I don't want it, but I'm stuck with the clients, and the firm is watching how I walk this damned tightrope."

"They can't expect you to win," Newton said. "There's no basis for it." Not from what he'd seen. "They're only making her life harder. The judge is going to see that and isn't going to be sympathetic to their cause at all, especially given what their son has done."

"Sometimes 'winning' is simply an outcome that doesn't make the firm look bad. The partners took this case, and now we're stuck with it. They thought it was going to be a groundbreaking situation to assert the rights of grandparents. But it's just a mess." Chase groaned as he laid his head back.

"Then the solution is simple. Make your clients see reality. Make it harsh and as personal to them as you can." Newton took Chase's hand. "Give them something that they could really lose. They're so intent on winning that there's the chance they could lose everything." He met Chase's gaze, and he nodded.

"I came close to it." He leaned in to kiss him. "I know I'm a smart guy, but sometimes I can be really dumb."

"Fear does strange things to us." Newton was about to stand, but stayed where he was instead. "You scared me, Chase. I didn't think I was ever going to find someone who would accept me and my issues, as well as the fact that I have kids. But I did, and when I wondered if that was gone...."

"It wasn't. I needed a little time to come to my senses. I've only had my career for so long that when I thought it could have been threatened, I retrenched, and I did it badly, I know that. I've always done it. Mom says it's because of what happened to me. When I'm under threat, I retreat back behind my walls, and I didn't see it. But she's right. Some people build walls and hide behind them. I did the same, but I put mine on wheels so they're always with me." Chase lowered his gaze, staring at the floor. "I guess I thought I was over all of that."

Newton patted his hand. "We never get over it. All we do is learn to live with what happened." He was living proof of that. "How about we agree to talk before we overreact, okay?" He smiled slightly.

"I think I can do that." Chase drew closer once again. "What I need to do is remember what's truly important."

"I know your job has been the center of your life and...."

"That's not what I meant." Chase kissed him, nearly sending Newton sprawling back on the sofa with the intensity. "I spent a lot of time trying to justify what I thought I wanted. Even Milton noticed that I was preoccupied, and that was embarrassing. I passed it off as being deep in thought about a case, but I kept thinking about you, Rosie, and Eric." He took Newton's hand. "I know it's pretty early, but I want you and those two precious kids to be my family. This house... and you... all of you feel like home to me."

"You feel like home to us too," Newton said. "Rosie even said that if you came over and wanted to kiss, she wouldn't even watch." He smiled. "So, what exactly are you proposing, counselor?"

"I'm saying that I love you, Newton, and I want to be part of your life, and Rosie's and Eric's. I want to be here for you, and have you be there for me." Chase sighed and swallowed. "I know you and I need to take things at a reasonable pace. It isn't just you and me. But I wanted to ask if you'd be willing to give it a try." He blinked. "That's what's really important—you and the kids... us... a family."

Newton's mouth hung open. This wasn't at all how he had expected this conversation to go. Hell, just half an hour ago he had been bracing for something bad, and now Chase was asking him to be his boyfriend… for the two of them to build a family. And Chase loved him.

"You really love me?"

"Yeah. I do, and you don't have to say it back just because I said it. Sometimes love, deep love, takes time… and I want to give that a chance for us."

"I want that too," Newton whispered around the lump in his throat. "I gave up on something like this a long time ago." He looked down at his gimpy foot. "I guess sometimes when you least expect it, love just shows up." Newton got to his feet, leaning on Chase as he led the way up the stairs to his room. This was almost like a dream, and Newton hoped it lasted forever.

CHAPTER 8

CHASE PASSED into Milton's office and shook his hand before sitting across from him. "The Anderson case is finished." He handed him the file. "Our clients have agreed to drop their claims, which had no merit and were discredited by multiple Social Services visits. The initial hearing didn't go their way at all, and unfortunately at that point, they were even more determined. These were people filled with hate, and they were trying to use us as a weapon against their former daughter-in-law."

"Okay, then," Milton said with a smile. "What did you say to make this happen?"

"I didn't say anything. But it seemed that Child Services did receive a call about their petition—probably from the court, though it could have been someone else—and decided that they needed to weigh in on the potential living environment for this little boy. One of their agents inspected the grandparents' house and found a room made up for their son, the boy's father. After that, Child Services saw the handwriting on the wall." Chase grinned and sat back in the chair. "For the record, I didn't make that call. But they finally saw reason and decided it was best if they tried to work things out with the ex-daughter-in-law."

"No. I'm sure you didn't. But you saved the firm some embarrassment and loss of prestige by getting this handled and off our books."

"Yes, and I suggest that for anything in the future, the Andersons be told they should seek other representation. This case was a loser from the start." And it had almost cost Chase dearly. Thank goodness Newton was clearheaded. "I also need to explain that I am dating someone." He reached into the file and pulled out a copy of the Child Services report. "Him. The author of that report is my boyfriend. He has two children, and I adore both of them. I want you to know so there is no conflict of interest."

"I see," Milton hummed. "I don't see where there would be. They are independent, and they manage their own work. We have no influence over the agency and would never exert any."

"Very true. But I don't want any connection with Newton and myself to be a secret." Chase leaned forward. "I also need to explain something to you. I know that I am being considered for partner, and you know that's what I want. But...." His train of thought wandered a second. "I also want to have a family and people who love me, and if push comes to shove, they will come first. This is a business—they are life. I don't want to wake up twenty years from now with three divorces behind me, living in my house alone, with only my briefs to keep me company. I'm a good lawyer... one of the best family law attorneys in the state."

Milton nodded. "Yes, you are."

"Do you know why?"

"You're gifted and—" Milton began.

Chase shook his head. "I was on the other side of the case as a child. I was abused by my father, and no child, no matter what, should ever be put in that position. I'm a good attorney because I fight for the children and will always take their side. I won't be put in the position to go against everything I stand for and believe again. These people were despicable, and while they are entitled to representation if they want it, let them look somewhere else other than to me and to us. We're better than that. No one wins every time, but I damned well want to try to make sure that it's the children that win no matter what."

"What are you saying?" Milton asked, furrowing his brow.

"That partner or not, from here on out, I will have a voice in the family law cases that this firm takes. I'm best qualified to assess and make sure that the clients we take are best for the firm. We don't want to find ourselves on the despicable side of a case again."

"And it's best for you?" Milton raised his eyebrows.

"What's best for me as an attorney is also what's best for the firm. My prestige is the firm's prestige. You know that." Chase left the implication that he could leave and start his own firm, and that the partners had screwed the pooch on this case, unsaid.

"Good." Milton smiled. "I like associates who look out for the firm." It was a dismissal, and Chase stood. "Just to be clear, I agree with you. I will take your suggestion up with the other partners, but I doubt we're going to have an issue." He smiled again as Chase left the office.

He ignored Hank's snicker and returned to his desk. He might have just blown his chances of making partner sky-high, or he could have solidified them. He wasn't sure which, but he had been honest with Milton, and he hoped that counted for something.

His phone vibrated in his pocket as he passed William's desk.

How is your day? Newton's text read.

Chase smiled. *Getting better. How are you?*

The last two and a half weeks had been busy for both of them. Chase was glad it was Friday and his workload was clear. He'd been invited to go with Newton and the family on Saturday to the start of the Great Pumpkin Festival in Whitefish Bay. They brought in a bunch of pumpkins, and kids could carve them, and then they were put on display and lit in the park. They ended up with thousands of jack-o'-lanterns by Halloween.

Pretty good. I'll be leaving soon and will meet the kids when they get off the bus. After work, are you coming to dinner and staying for breakfast on Saturday? There were a bunch of naughty smiles after the message.

I already have a bag in the trunk. Have a few errands to run tomorrow. He sent the message and placed his phone on his desk.

"Now that's the smile of a contented man in *lurv*," William drolled with a grin. "So, do you think you can find me someone to make me look as sappy as all that?"

Chase rolled his eyes. "Did you need something, or did you come in here just to make trouble?"

"I was wondering if I can leave in an hour? My mom and dad are coming to town, and I need to meet them and figure out how we're going to clean up the latest mess my brother has made for them." The trouble and ache that shone in his eyes was enough for Chase to nod.

"And be sure to have some fun this weekend," Chase said. "Newton and I are taking the kids to the pumpkin festival. You and your parents are welcome to join us if you want some time outside."

William sighed. Chase hated seeing him this down. He was usually a ray of sunshine in an office that could be a pressure cooker. "I don't think I should. This weekend isn't going to be fun, and I'm going to have to try to keep my mom from having a nervous breakdown. Samuel is a handful, and he's gotten himself into trouble. Honestly, I'd ask for help, but they're down in Illinois and things are different."

Chase nodded. "Is it legal trouble?"

"Legal, financial. My mom and dad are beside themselves." William closed the door. "I think they're finally going to have to let him sink or swim on his own. But it's hard to tell them that. He's older than I am, and he has to deal with the consequences of his actions." William pulled open the door.

"If there's anything I can do...."

"I know, Chase. And thank you." William forced a smile and returned to his desk. Chase hoped things worked out for him. He didn't want to lose William and was already fighting to get him a raise, because he was worth it.

Chase took a couple of phone meetings that afternoon, and said goodbye to William when he left, knowing he'd help if William asked. He finished up for the week, having the entire weekend free, and drove to Newton's. He opened the front door and stepped in to tears. Rosie was crying, and Newton lay on the floor, tears running down his cheeks.

"Where's Eric?" Chase asked as the boy ran in with a bag of ice and handed it to Newton.

"Daddy's foot looks funny," Rosie said, and Chase knelt down next to Newton, lifting the blanket. His foot was red, going to purple.

"I'm okay. Just help me to the sofa," Newton said.

Chase lifted him up and got him sat down. "Rosie, get your jacket on, and Eric, grab your bag. Make sure there are snacks in it for both of you, then get in your dad's car."

"Where are we going?"

"We're taking Daddy to the hospital." There was no way in hell Chase was messing around with this. Newton's foot didn't look good at all. It was very swollen, and even when it was sprained, it hadn't looked this bad. It seemed to Chase that there was blood pooling in the foot and starting to darken.

"I'm fine," Newton protested, then winced.

Rosie had her jacket on, and Chase hugged her before lifting her into his arms. "Eric, are you ready?" He opened the door and carried Rosie to the car while Eric followed. He got them settled in the back seat and returned for Newton, who was being completely stubborn.

"Your foot is going to turn black. It has to have someone look at it. You've fought and dealt with the pain for years. Do you want to lose it now?" All Chase could think of was that if the foot was badly infected, it could spread and then he could lose Newton forever. "We need to have it looked at and taken care of." Chase leaned closer. "I love you and hate seeing you in pain. So, humor me and let me see to it that you're taken care of."

Chase half carried Newton to the car and got him into the passenger seat before speeding off toward the city.

Every few minutes he glanced at Newton, who had pain etched in the lines around his eyes. He was trying to cover it up, but Chase saw it clearly. When he hit a bump in the pavement, Newton hissed. His foot was a lot more painful than Newton was trying to admit, and that only confirmed Chase had made the right decision.

"Is Daddy going to be okay?" Rosie asked.

"Yes. I'm going to be just fine," Newton said.

Chase wasn't so sure. Newton was growing pale, and Chase wondered if he was running a fever when beads of sweat broke out in the otherwise cool interior.

Chase was relieved when the left turn into Emergency appeared. He pulled right up. "Okay, guys. Let's get your dad inside, and then I can come out to move the car while you watch over him." He hurried and got Newton out and moved inside, with the kids right behind like they expected to be left. Chase helped Newton to the intake desk, explained what was going on, and sat Newton into a chair. "You give them the details, and don't try to make light of it," he gently scolded, then hurried out to park the car.

By the time he returned, Newton was in a chair with his foot propped up, a worried child on either side of him. Chase approached the desk to see what was going on.

"He'll be called in turn."

"I know you have protocols and things, but that man was on the scene at 9-11, and the issues with his foot stem from that. He's been through hell, and if something happens, you don't want it on the evening news that a first responder to the worst terrorist attack in the country's history was kept waiting in an emergency room." Chase met her now-worried gaze and then turned away.

"Mr. DeSantis," a woman called minutes later.

Chase transferred Newton to the wheelchair he'd gotten and brought him back. They took him to an intake room, and then, after getting vitals, brought Newton to a large room and got him settled in a bed. Chase sat in one of the chairs, with Rosie climbing onto his lap and Eric sitting on the other side of the bed.

Eric got Newton some water and otherwise sat still in the chair. "It's okay, Dad. They're probably going to order an MRI of your foot and maybe X-rays. Though an MRI is a better bet because it shows more." Chase figured Eric had been through enough hospitals to know the routine.

"You can sit next to your dad if you want," Chase offered. This wasn't what any of them had expected for the evening, and Chase wanted to keep the kids occupied. There was going to be plenty of waiting around. Eric was still, and Rosie pressed to him, holding him tight, fear rolling off her little body as they sat without saying a word.

The doctor entered, introduced himself, and lifted the blanket to look at Newton's foot. It was pretty obvious that he tried not to react, but failed. A nurse entered right behind him. "I want an MRI, and I want him first in line. Get an orderly to take him down." He turned to Newton. "Your foot is in bad shape. We're going to start an IV with antibiotics and get some images. Then we'll figure out what's happening and what we're going to do from there."

"Thank you," Chase said, sharing a hard look with Newton. "He seems to think this is no big deal."

"We'll see what's going on and find out how big a deal it is."

"Thank you," Newton said, and the doctor left.

"It's okay, Dad," Eric paid, patting Newton's hand. "It doesn't hurt too much when they put the IV in." He was the expert, after all.

The nurse got busy starting the fluids, and then once that was set, someone arrived to take Newton for his test. Chase and the kids stayed where they were, sitting nearly silently while they waited.

"Once they bring your dad back, we can go to the cafeteria and see about something to eat." He wasn't sure what there was going to be, but the kids had to have dinner of some sort.

Newton returned an hour later, and then they all waited for the results.

The doctor returned, looking grave.

"Eric, there's a soda machine just down the hall." Chase handed him some money. "Go get each of you some water and a bag of chips."

Eric took the money and then led Rosie out by the hand.

"They'll be gone a few minutes," Chase said, and took Newton's hand.

"Your foot is in bad shape. There is an abscess inside that is about to burst. The antibiotics will fight it, but we need to go in, clean it out, and see what other damage has been done. We need to do it now before it spreads any farther up your leg. The surgeon is already on his way in, and I have nurses set to prep you. I have to stress that this is imperative. There is no other choice if you want to try to save the foot and your life."

Chase squeezed his hand. "I'll be here through all of it, you know that." The thought of losing Newton scared him to his very core.

"But what if they take my foot?" Newton asked, his words barely above a whisper. "What if something happens to me? My mother will swoop in and try to take my children." He pushed back the bedding, and Chase stopped him.

"I'll be here no matter what. You need to relax and stay calm." Chase turned to the doctor and then back to Newton. "You have to do this, and I'll be here when you get back, and so will Rosie and

Eric, ready to see you and give you all the hugs and love they can. And if they have to take your foot, then the three of us will love you just the same."

Newton sighed and nodded. "Bring me the forms, and I'll sign them."

The doctor left the room, and a nurse returned with the consent forms. Newton signed them just as the kids returned. Rosie once again climbed onto Chase's lap, and Eric sat in the chair.

"Guys, I'm going to have to have surgery. I'm going to be okay. But when they come to get me, Chase is going to take both of you home. It will probably take a long time."

"We're going to stay here to be with you, Dad," Eric said, suddenly sounding much older than his nine years.

Newton extended his hand, and Eric took it. Rosie held the other one, and Newton closed his eyes. "It will be all right," he said softly.

"WE NEED to get him ready," a nurse said as she came in ten minutes later.

"I'm going to take these two down to get something to eat." Chase turned to the nurse. "Let's say goodbye and then we can get some food." Chase kissed Newton gently and then took the kids out of Emergency, following the signs to the exit.

Chase took the kids to McDonald's. None of them were particularly hungry, but Eric ate some and drank plenty. Rosie picked at her food, and Chase couldn't say much because his appetite was nowhere to be found. His phone chimed that they were taking Newton in a few minutes, so he took the kids back, and they all said goodbye to a very groggy Newton before watching as he was wheeled away.

"It's going to be hours," Chase said. "Why don't I bring you home." He wasn't sure what he was going to do once he got there. If things were different, he'd call Newton's mom to stay with them, but that wasn't an option.

"I want to see Daddy when he comes back," Rosie whined, and began to cry.

Chase lifted her into his arms, hugging her tightly. "You will see him. I promise you." He led the way out and to the parking area.

There was nothing he could do now other than wait, and they could do that much better at home. He got them to the car, with Rosie still whimpering and probably mad at him, but Chase had to do what they needed. Once they were buckled in, he fished through his phone and made a call.

"Jolene," Chase said when she answered.

"Man, something must be bad if you're calling me."

"Newton's in the hospital, and he has to have emergency surgery on his foot. I need to be there for him and I have the kids, and...." Chase was a little overwhelmed. How parents managed to be in two or three places at once was beyond him.

"I'm on a call. But I'll stop by the house as soon as I can, and bring Kirsten and Stevie with me. They know both kids."

"Thank you." Chase felt stretched thin.

"No problem. Give me half an hour or so." She hung up, and Chase started the car, driving back to Newton's house.

Both kids trudged up the walk like they had concrete in their shoes. Chase didn't feel so hot either. "Jolene and the kids are going to come over."

"Is she babysitting us?" Eric asked as though it was a bad word.

Chase used the key Newton had given him to unlock the house, and they went inside. "Hang up your jackets, and we'll talk on the sofa." He sat and waited until Rosie joined him, and then Eric. "Okay. Your dad is really sick. He's having surgery so they can fix his foot. Jolene is going to come over so that when your dad wakes up, I can be there with him and he isn't alone. I want both of you to promise me that you'll be good for her and that you'll go to bed when she says. I promise I'll come see you when I get back, and tomorrow we'll go see your dad." He hoped he was doing the right thing by being honest with them. They deserved straight answers.

"What if Daddy dies?" Rosie asked.

Oh God. "Your daddy is going to be just fine." But her question set off bells in the back of his head. He needed to make sure the kids were taken care of if something did happen. He didn't want to think about that now. "I promise you'll see your daddy tomorrow, and if I hear anything from the hospital, I promise to tell you."

The doorbell rang, and Rosie slipped off his lap to answer it. Jolene came in with her Stevie and Kirsten, and the four kids went into the family room to play. Chase stood to greet her and offered a chair.

"How is he?"

"The foot is bad. There could be gangrene or God knows what. It was huge, and the infection would have spread without the surgery. I can't tell you how much I appreciate you coming over. I wasn't sure who else to call."

"Sweetheart, go on back to the hospital. You did the right thing. Just make sure he's okay, and I'll call in to the office so they know that he's likely to be out for a while." Jolene patted his hand. "That man has been through hell, as I'm sure you know. He's as strong as an ox, with twice the determination. Go be with him. Newton has spent years alone, and he needs to know that he has someone to be there for him. I'll be here if you need anything."

"Thank you." Chase got his jacket and went into the other room, where the girls were on the floor playing doll truck drivers. Eric and Stevie sat on the sofa with their games. "I'll call you, I promise." He said goodbye and left the house to drive back to the hospital.

He parked and went inside as his phone vibrated. Newton was out of surgery and in recovery. He followed the directions from the lady at the desk and found Newton in recovery. Chase held his hand while he waited for him to wake up.

"Are you Chase?" the nurse asked. "He was asking for you a few minutes ago, but he went back to sleep. The anesthesia is still working out of his system."

"Did you call his mother?" Chase asked, not knowing what arrangements had been set up, and hoping like hell that he wasn't going to have to fight with her right there in the hospital.

"She was listed as his emergency contact, so someone has most likely telephoned her. I'm not sure." Zinya, as her name tag read, returned to taking care of Newton.

Chase stepped out to call Jolene.

"Is he awake?" Jolene asked.

"Not really. He's still out of it, but they probably called his mother. If she shows up, don't let her in the house. Newton has been having a ton of trouble with her, and she'll try to take the kids. Tell her to come here if she does." He and Newton could deal with her once he was awake.

"Will do. Everything is quiet, and I put on a movie. Rosie is half asleep on the sofa, and Eric is playing his game. I swear he'd get lost in that thing." She didn't sound upset, and Chase was about to go back inside when Newton's mother breezed up to him. He ended the call quickly.

"I should have known you'd be here. Go on home and stay away from him. I'm family, and you aren't welcome." She went inside, pointedly closing the door.

Chase followed anyway and up to Newton's bed. His mother was issuing instructions to the staff that he wasn't supposed to be there, but Chase ignored her for the moment, leaning over the bed.

"Hey, it's good to see those pretty eyes of yours," Chase said. "How are you feeling?"

"Ma'am, we need to do our jobs."

"Mrs. DeSantis, you need to leave," Chase said calmly. "You're the one who isn't welcome." He held Newton's hand.

"Mother." Newton's voice was raspy and very soft.

"Yes, baby," she cooed, and approached the bed like she was mother of the year.

"Go home," Newton said very clearly, and closed his eyes. "Just leave me alone."

"That's good enough for me," a nurse said. "You need to leave, or I'll call security and have you escorted out." She was fierce, and Chase was grateful for it.

Mrs. DeSantis finally turned to leave, and Chase followed her out. "I'm going to get those children, and…." Her eyes blazed with righteous indignation.

"You come near the house and the police will be called. The kids are with a friend, and she has instructions. You aren't allowed inside or on the property. A restraining order is in effect, and you received a copy."

She narrowed her eyes and looked seconds from hauling off and punching him.

Chase didn't back down. "Newton is an amazing man. He's caring and thoughtful, and he adores his family and will do anything for them. You're only hurting him with this crusade of yours. He deserves to be able to lead his own life, not one that somehow lives up to your standards. The only thing you get to decide is if you're going to be part of his life or not."

She stood a little taller. "I'm his mother, and...."

Chase scowled and lowered his voice. Clearly, she had heard nothing he'd said and was lost in her own view of the world. "For all the hurt you've caused him, I'd love to get you in court." He smiled as menacingly as he knew he could. "Just try me—I'll rip you to shreds." Then he turned, ignoring her indignation as he went back to Newton, who was more awake.

"Is my foot still there?" Newton asked.

"Yes. You still have two. I don't know what the doctor had to do, but it's still there, and you're back with me. That's what matters." Chase once again held Newton's hand. "Jolene is home with the kids, and they're going to be happy to know you're okay." He was thrilled and relieved, more than words could express.

The nurse checked Newton's pain level and gave him something. He slowly became more and more awake. "They'll take him up to a room pretty soon. I expect the surgeon to be in too."

The surgeon, Dr. Grantham, made an appearance.

"Young man, you were very lucky. That sprain you had a few weeks ago created an abscess in your foot, and it had expanded quite a bit. We got to it before it burst, and we were able to clean out the infection. If it had burst, it would be a completely different story. I was also able to repair some of the earlier damage to the foot."

"What does that mean?" Chase asked, lightly squeezing Newton's hand. He was so damned grateful that Newton was going to be all right. That was all that truly mattered.

"That when he heals, and after he has weeks off his feet, he should have the use of his foot again. And if he truly lets it heal, it might be stronger. But I want to stress that there are no guarantees. There was little I could do with much of the damage,

and the pain is something you are still going to have to live with."
He smiled. "Let the people who care about you take care of you."
Chase thanked him.

"Hear that? You need to let us help... all of us."

"But...."

"I know you're used to helping everyone else, but you need
to stop overdoing it and let us take care of you sometimes." Chase
brought Newton's hand to his lips, kissing the back. "I want you
around for a very long time." His voice broke and he stood right next
to Newton, needing the closeness. "Promise me...."

"I'll try," Newton whispered and Chase took that as the best
answer he was going to get. Not that he intended to let the topic go
permanently.

Chase held Newton's hand until they came to take him to a
room. Then he walked right next to him as they transported him down
the halls and into a darkened space.

"Where are the kids?" Newton asked.

Chase figured he didn't remember and explained again. "I'm
going to go be with them in a little while, but I'll bring them in to see
you tomorrow. I promise." He doubted he could actually keep them
away if he tried.

"Okay," Newton whispered while the nurse got him settled and
made sure he had enough blankets. Chase kissed him goodbye and
gently touched his forehead before leaving the room once Newton
had drifted off to sleep.

He made it to the hallway and into the elevator before breaking
down in tears of sheer relief.

"WE HAVE to be quiet. There are a lot of people here who need
their rest," Chase told Rosie as she practically skipped down the
hospital hallway the following morning. When the three of them
reached Newton's room, they went inside, Rosie hurrying up to
the bed.

"Daddy, I made this for you." She handed a groggy Newton the
picture she'd drawn for him. "It's the pumpkin I want to carve. Mr.
Chase said we can do that when you get home." She balanced on her

tiptoes so she could get closer to Newton. Eric stood on the other side of the bed.

"How are you, son?" Newton asked. "Did you take all your medicine?"

"Yes. And I didn't complain when I drank the stuff." Eric didn't even make a face when he talked about it. He was growing up, and Chase saw that realization in Newton's eyes. It was pride and a great deal of love shining there for both of them. Hell, when Newton's gaze shifted to Chase, it didn't change. That love was still there—intensified and different, but there.

"You're getting to be so big, and soon you'll be all grown up," Newton said softly. "Both of you will." He smiled, and Chase stepped nearer.

"Has the doctor been in this morning?"

"No, not yet. Hopefully it'll be soon. I hope I can go home today." They still had the IV running into Newton's arm, and Chase figured that was a little optimistic.

"You just rest. I thought that this afternoon, I'd take the kids to the pumpkin festival so they could carve their pumpkins and have a little fun." This whole incident had left Chase a little off-balance. He was lucky; they all were. Chase had finally found someone to love and hold, and he'd come very close to losing him. Newton might try to make light of it, but Chase knew in his heart what he'd found and nearly lost just like that. He sighed and moved closer to the bed, taking Newton's hand.

"Have you been good for Chase?" Newton asked Rosie.

"Yes. He took us to McDonald's for breakfast." Rosie leaned nearer.

Newton smiled, fatigue settling in around his eyes.

"Guys, we have to be quiet," Chase reminded them, and sat down. Rosie climbed onto his lap the way she usually did and sat remarkably quietly. "Are you in a lot of pain?"

"Yeah. The foot aches and sometimes throbs. They're giving me things for it, but I'm used to discomfort. I'm just happy they were able to save it."

"Yes, we were," the surgeon said as he came in the room.

"Chase, and this is Rosie and Eric," Chase introduced them all. "Thank you for helping him."

The doctor smiled and turned to Newton. "You gave us quite a challenge. We believe we got all of the infection, and we've got you on antibiotics to make sure. We'll most likely switch to oral ones later today. But you need to take better care of yourself. That foot is going to need attention, and as it heals, I want you to take it easy. Elevate it and let it rest. If you do that, things should be better for you than they have been in a while."

"Thank you."

"Newton has been living with pain and discomfort for a long time," Chase supplied. Newton put everyone else first and took care of himself last. That was something that Chase needed to change. Or if nothing else, Chase was going to make sure that Newton came first with him.

"I'm sure he has. But hopefully he'll get some relief now." The doctor checked over the incision while Chase kept the kids busy on the other side of the hanging curtain. When he pushed the curtain back, Rosie hurried to the doctor.

"When can my daddy come home?" She looked up at him, and Chase stifled a laugh. No one could resist that look, and heaven help whoever eventually married her.

"Probably tomorrow, I think." He smiled and spoke some more with Newton.

By the time the doctor left, Newton was growing tired. He didn't seem to want to sleep and talked with the kids, but his eyes kept drifting closed even as Rosie told him all about the things she and Kirsten had done the night before.

"Why don't you two put your jackets on, and we'll get ready to go." Chase leaned over the bed while Rosie and Eric were occupied. "I really miss you and didn't sleep at all last night."

"Why?"

"Because you weren't there." Chase grinned. "I'm ready for you to come home and feel better so you and I can have a little adult fun time." He winked, and Newton groaned. Chase lowered his gaze to the slight bulge in the sheets. "Well, part of you is feeling better," he whispered before kissing him. "I love you, and once you get home, I intend to show you just how much."

Newton whimpered. Rosie's whine and Eric groaning, the surefire start to an argument, pulled away his attention. "Thank you for taking care of them."

"We're a family," Chase said, squeezing Newton's hand. "And right now we're missing the most important member, so get better so you can come home." That was all he wanted—for their family to be whole again. He kissed him, and after a quiet goodbye, he took Rosie and Eric and left the hospital.

THAT NIGHT, Chase tossed and turned. He couldn't sleep because Newton wasn't there. It felt strange to be sleeping in his house without him. At home Chase did all right at night, but at Newton's, his mind was programmed to have him there.

Eventually he got up, because staying in bed wasn't doing him any good. He reached for his phone and sent a text to his mom. He wasn't at all surprised when he got an answer. She was a night owl and often read well into the evening.

Why are you up this late? she texted.

Stuff is happening and I can't sleep.

His phone vibrated, and he answered it, smiling at her voice.

"What's going on? Does it have to do with Newton and his kids?"

"Yes and no." It was an enigmatic answer, but Chase was so very turned around at the moment. "Newton is in the hospital because of his foot. He had emergency surgery, but he's going to be fine." Chase sighed.

"You should have called me. Do you need help with the kids? I can check on a flight and come help." That was his mom. They might not be in each other's pockets, but she was there if he needed her.

"It's not that." Chase tried to put his discomfort and unease into words. "I love him, Mom. I really do. When he was hurting, it tore at my heart, and now I'm awake, scared, and worried, and… I know he's going to be fine, but I'm still scared." He'd finally been able to admit that to someone.

"Of course, you are. Honey, you went through a lot as a child, and it took me a long time to get over my guilt for letting it happen. When your dad hurt you, he ripped away your security, and you had to protect yourself."

Chase nodded. "And I let my guard down with Newton." Suddenly it was so clear. "I let him in, and I'm scared to death that I'm going to lose him." He could see now how he'd allowed Newton to become the new center of his life. "For years my life was my job, and now it's him," he added, thinking out loud.

"Yes. That's exactly it, and this incident and the surgery scared you, but...." His mom sniffed. "I was beginning to think that you were never going to find someone. That what happened to you as a child was going to affect the rest of your life. It's okay to be scared and frightened for the ones you love. That just shows you how much they live in your heart." He could almost see his mom's smile. "Now you go to bed and get some sleep, because Newton is going to need you. And when he's better, Costas and I will arrange to come out to visit. I'm thinking Thanksgiving, if that works for both of you."

"Are you crying?" Chase asked.

"Who's crying?" Rosie asked as she came in the room in her Mulan nightgown.

"I'm talking to my mom," Chase said as Rosie climbed onto the bed. She held out her hand, and Chase figured what the hell and handed her the phone.

"Hi, I'm Rosie," she said with an unusual amount of cheer for just after midnight. The two of them chatted like old friends, with Rosie telling his mother all about her dolls. "Okay... okay... goodbye, Grandma Chase." She handed back the phone. "I need a drink of water, and is it morning yet so we can see Daddy?"

"Go get some water and go back to bed. I'll come tuck you in, and we'll see your daddy in the morning. We get to bring him home, but only if you go back to sleep." He smiled at her, and she slid off the bed to leave the room.

"Sorry, Mom," he said, and this time he was sure his mother was crying. "Mom...?"

She sniffed and blew her nose. "I'm a grandma." Her voice sounded shaky. "And you're a dad." She had just voiced one of his worst fears.

"Maybe that's what scares me," Chase admitted, and deep in the back of his mind, something snapped. He'd always read that the abused were likely to grow up to be abusers. And he felt that link break in that moment. He was *never* going to be what his father was.

CHAPTER 9

NEWTON CLOSED his eyes and gritted his teeth to keep from groaning. He'd been home exactly three hours, and Rosie, Eric, and Chase hovered over him like birds. Rosie insisted on sitting with her back pressed to his belly as though he was going to disappear if she couldn't touch him. Eric kept asking if he needed anything, and Chase came in every five minutes to check on him.

"Rosie, I'm not going anywhere." Newton lightly rubbed her back. "Go and play for a while, okay?" He was starting to feel a little boxed in.

Rosie looked to him, biting her lower lip, and then slipped off the sofa. She walked toward the other room like her feet were heavy, turning back to him before leaving the room. Newton figured she'd return to check on him every so often all afternoon.

Newton closed his eyes and did his best to get comfortable, but his foot ached. The pain wasn't sharp, but it was there, constantly. The meds reduced the intensity but didn't take it away completely.

"Here's your pill," Chase said, handing it to him, along with a glass of water.

"What is it?" Newton asked with a sigh.

"One of the prescriptions," Chase answered.

Newton waved it away. "No. Vicodin only makes me loopy and plugs me up so I can't go. Just give me some ibuprofen." He hated that prescription stuff. A few minutes of pain relief were not worth the awful side effects. Chase gave him an "Are you sure?" look and returned with what he asked for, along with fresh ice to keep the swelling down. Once Newton was comfortable again, he closed his eyes, and as the meds took effect, he slipped off to sleep.

His foot even ached in his dreams, only now it was worse, really bad, and he had a mask on so he could breathe better, but dust coated his mouth and nose. Doctors and nurses tried to help him, but

Newton fought them, not understanding anything. He rolled from side to side as people called his name, but he continued fighting. He had to get out of here, get away. He couldn't go through all that again.

"Newton!"

A sharp voice cut through, and Newton sat up, opening his eyes. He was home in his living room, and the scent of dust was gone. He took a deep breath and relaxed.

"You were there again, weren't you?" Chase sat next to him.

"Yeah. I had flashbacks the last time I had surgery. I keep thinking I'm not going to come back or that I have no control... or something."

"Maybe your head is just putting a whole bunch of things together, a sort of flashback soup," Chase offered.

Newton nodded. It was as good an explanation as any.

"Just relax as best you can. I'm here, and I'll stand watch over your dreams." He sat in the chair near the sofa. Of course things didn't work that way, but Newton liked that Chase was taking a stand for him. Maybe that was all he needed. Newton wasn't alone this time. He extended his hand, and Chase took it as Newton's fatigue once again overwhelmed him.

"NIGHT, DADDY," Rosie said, climbing onto the sofa to kiss him good night.

"Good night, honey. You sleep well, and I'll see you when you wake up." Newton hugged her. It was a little awkward, but he'd managed to sit up and wrap his arms around his little girl. Once she climbed down, he gave Eric a hug as well, and then Chase took them both upstairs. Newton lay quietly, wishing he could be up there tucking them in, but Chase seemed to be doing a great job, and a few giggles reached his ears.

When Chase returned, Newton patted the seat next to him. "Thank you for everything. The way you stepped in with them was amazing. They really love you."

Chase tugged him closer, and Newton leaned against him. "I love them too, and I really love their dad, a whole lot. Like with my entire heart." He moved closer to Newton, kissing him gently at first, but with increasing passion. "I missed you so much. You scared me half to death."

"I missed you too, and I love you just as much. I know it's dumb, but before you, I thought I had all the love that I needed in my life. I was wrong." Newton returned the kiss, holding Chase tightly, the ache in his foot receding to nothing. It seemed Chase's affections were stronger than pain meds. Chase was the drug he'd happily become dependent on for the rest of his life.

"Do you want to watch a movie?" Chase asked once he sat back up.

"No. I think I want to sit here in the quiet with you and just be." Newton leaned his head on Chase's shoulder, soaking in the warmth and closeness of his lover.

He must have dozed off for a while and jerked awake to soft chuckles from Chase, who didn't seem to mind. "I think I should go up to bed."

"Okay." Chase stood and got Newton's crutches, turned out the lights, and walked with him as Newton made his way up the stairs. He was so happy to see his own bed, it was beyond words. He used the bathroom and washed up, then let Chase help him out of his clothes and with climbing into bed. Newton sighed as warmth and comfort surrounded him, and when Chase joined him, the comfort and heat only increased. Chase darkened the room, and Newton got comfortable but ended up staring at the ceiling.

"I slept too damned much today," Newton said with a yawn that didn't portend him falling to sleep.

"All right." Chase slipped out of bed, locked the door, and climbed back onto the mattress, tugging away the covers. The cool air kissed Newton's skin, and he hissed slightly. Chase got the oil out of the nightstand and worked it onto his hands. Newton closed his eyes as Chase massaged his chest and shoulders. He breathed deeply, letting the tension slip away.

"You have magic hands," Newton said softly. "And lips," he added as Chase kissed his shoulder. "Dang, that feels so good."

"I hope so," Chase whispered in his ear, sucking lightly on the lobe. "I want it to." He kissed Newton again, licking at the base of his neck, Chase's hands never stopping their ministrations. "I want you to forget about your foot and everything else for just a few minutes. Let the pain go, and concentrate on my hands." As Chase said that, his hands slid lower, right along Newton's cock, which instantly took a vivid interest. "Don't move."

"Chase...."

"That's it. Keep your eyes closed and your body still."

"Can I do this?" Newton slid his hand down Chase's leg and wrapped his fingers around Chase's shaft, stroking with his hand.

"Yes...," Chase hissed without stopping. He continued the massage, long slow strokes down Newton's chest and belly, to his cock, adding desire and need, letting them build so slowly that Newton wanted to scream, but he didn't dare. "You're so beautiful, Newton, just like this. And all mine."

Chase's hands moved a little faster, his strokes a little more forceful, desire rising at the base of his skull, pressure building in his spine. He didn't try to stop it, letting the pleasure overwhelm him, soaking him in heat and warmth that increased with each stroke. Newton clamped his eyes closed, letting Chase have him, body and soul. It was the most natural thing in the world.

"I love you, Newton. You're the center of my world."

And just like that, Newton could take no more and let go of everything, gasping as Chase kissed him while his body throbbed with sweet abandon.

Newton couldn't move. Not that he needed to. Chase took care of him, washing, drying, and then pulling up the covers before climbing in himself.

"Chase, I want to tell you something before I go to sleep." He didn't roll over because he was perfectly comfortable. "I don't want you to leave us... ever. Will you stay?" His fatigue was catching up with him.

"For always?" Chase asked.

"Yes, for always. Be my love and my life."

"Only if you'll be mine," Chase said, and Newton held his hand, kissing the back of it. "Should I draw up a contract?"

Newton snickered and leaned nearer, sealing their covenant with a kiss.

EPILOGUE

THE WIND blew off the water, and the others around Newton bundled up against the cold as they either milled though the memorial park or rushed under the leafless trees past the depressions that represented where the towers had once stood. Newton wandered around each one and ran his fingers over the letters of his friend Carmello's name carved in the steel that edged the waterfall pool. When he found Anthony's name, Newton paused, tracing each letter. Tears ran down his cheeks as he played his message for the last time. Then Newton sent the recording to Chase to give to the museum, and deleted it from his phone. He had removed it from all his other devices before this trip.

"Are you sure you want to do this?" Chase asked from next to him, an arm around his shoulders, holding him tightly.

"Yes. I have to do this. I need to say goodbye and put this part of my life behind me to be able to move forward." Newton shivered as he stared down into the imprint of the North Tower, the water cascading over the edge and along the bottom before disappearing into the final drop in the center. "I know what happened to me will always be part of my life, but it can't be what defines me." He turned to Chase. "I have so much in my life that's good. You, the kids, my job—everything—and this keeps hanging over my head. I have to let it go." Newton took Chase's hand and squeezed it hard before taking a step away from the pool. He turned toward the museum and took a deep breath. "Thank you for coming here with me, and when we get back, I have to thank your mom and dad for watching the kids."

Chase chuckled as a gust of wind cut through his coat. "Mom is so thrilled to be a grandmother. It's something she didn't expect. So when we get back, don't be surprised if Mom has taken them to FAO Schwartz, Bloomingdales, and possibly skating in Rockefeller Center. She was so excited."

"I love your mom and dad," Newton said. Chase had called Costas "Dad," so that was how Newton thought of him.

"They were disappointed we weren't able to come for Christmas because of the weather. They wanted to celebrate the holidays with us, as well as my making partner." A huge storm had socked in much of the Midwest, and they couldn't get out. "I think she's trying to make up for it all now."

Newton hoped she didn't spoil them too much, but with Eric and Rosie both calling them Grandma and Pa-pou, he figured there was some spoiling that was just going to happen. Costas didn't have children of his own, so these were their only grandchildren. Newton had reveled at the delight in Costas's eyes when Rosie asked him to teach her something in Greek.

"Are you ready to go?" Chase asked, probably because the wind was fierce and he was just as cold as Newton was.

"Let's get this over with." Newton wasn't sure what he expected from the museum, but what he didn't expect was the open atrium filled with light around the two tridents that had been part of the building exterior. Chase held his hand as they went deeper past the slurry wall, as well as the twisted piece of steel where the plane had actually hit. He was afraid to close his eyes in case he took a trip back almost eighteen years, and yet part of him was afraid to look. He had seen all of this and lived through it. Things were cleaner now, and in a museum, but he knew what they were and had once been.

"It's okay. We can go whenever you want," Chase told him.

"I know." Newton walked slowly through the exhibits and remnants of the building before entering the display of artifacts. Pieces of plane, the parts of people's lives. Newton exhaled softly. He was doing okay and was kind of proud of himself... until he turned that corner.

There in front of him was himself. A picture of him outside the partially ruined converted ambulance, covered in dust and dirt, with water bottles in his hands. Newton stilled, staring. He didn't quite know how to process being confronted with his own image on that first day. No mask, skin and clothes gray, hair chalked with dust.

"Sweetheart," Chase said, but Newton barely heard him. It was like he was in a fog.

"Excuse me," a woman said softly, and Newton was gently led away.

He wasn't sure what was happening, but the lady and Chase led him through a door he hadn't noticed and into a dimly lit room with large, comfortable chairs.

"Please make yourselves comfortable, and take as much time as you like." She pressed some water into his hand, and Newton looked down at the bottle, grateful it wasn't Dasani. People thought bottled water tasted the same, but Newton could never drink that again. It was all he'd had for three months, and the taste took him back instantly.

"Thank you," Chase said, and Newton nodded a little blankly.

"These rooms are for people like you, the survivors. There's nothing to be ashamed of. This happens quite a bit here, which is why we have these rooms, so you can have some quiet."

Newton lifted his gaze and smiled at her. She was probably fifty, with graying hair, warm eyes, and a kind face. "I wasn't expecting to see that," he said, finding his voice.

"We understand. Would you like us to remove the picture?" she asked. "We will be happy to. This museum represents something traumatic and terrible, but we want it to cause as little pain and hurt for those who experienced it as possible."

Newton shook his head. "That is as much a part of what happened as anything else. Please don't."

"Damn," Chase whispered from next to him.

"Would you like a copy of it? I will be happy to have one made and sent to you." She spoke barely above a whisper.

"Would you?" Newton asked, and turned to Chase. "I think that someday I'd like to be able to talk to the kids about what happened, and they might need to see me and what it looked like." He certainly wasn't going to frame it and put it up on the wall.

"Of course. You stay here as long as you like."

Chase handed her a card and explained the details. Then she exited the room, leaving them alone. "You are the strongest person I have ever met." Chase sniffed. "I don't know if I could have done what you just did."

"I had to." Newton lifted his gaze from where it had settled on the floor. "I need to heal and confront what happened. Then I can put more of this behind me." That was his hope, and already he felt better. Newton had been worried about how he was going to react to what he saw, and a few minutes ago, he had seen probably the most difficult image possible and he'd been okay. There was no flashback, only shock, and he could deal with that.

Chase stood, then leaned down and hugged him. "I'm so damn proud of you. Sometimes you really blow me away." He kissed him, and Newton held him in return, feeling much better, like he could really do this.

The woman returned and gave them information on the picture and when it would be sent. Newton thanked her, and she led them back to the museum, where he and Chase looked at the rest and then made their way out. There was no more drama from that point on.

Newton felt relieved when the bracing wind hit his face. He lifted his gaze upward to the new One World Trade Center, took a deep breath, and let the winter sun shine on his face. "Let's go," he said softly. "I need to see the kids and spend some time with you." He turned around. "That was the past, and it needs to stay there. You, Eric, and Rosie are the future." Newton pulled Chase to him, kissing him hard right out on the plaza, his love, his life, and his future on display.

When he pulled back, they shared a smile, and then he took Chase's hand, walked to the edge of the plaza, and hailed a taxi, ready for the rest of their lives.

ANDREW GREY is the author of more than one hundred works of Contemporary Gay Romantic fiction. After twenty-seven years in corporate America, he has now settled down in Central Pennsylvania with his husband, Dominic, and his laptop. An interesting ménage. Andrew grew up in western Michigan with a father who loved to tell stories and a mother who loved to read them. Since then he has lived throughout the country and traveled throughout the world. He is a recipient of the RWA Centennial Award, has a master's degree from the University of Wisconsin–Milwaukee, and now writes full-time. Andrew's hobbies include collecting antiques, gardening, and leaving his dirty dishes anywhere but in the sink (particularly when writing). He considers himself blessed with an accepting family, fantastic friends, and the world's most supportive and loving partner. Andrew currently lives in beautiful, historic Carlisle, Pennsylvania.

Email: andrewgrey@comcast.net
Website: www.andrewgreybooks.com

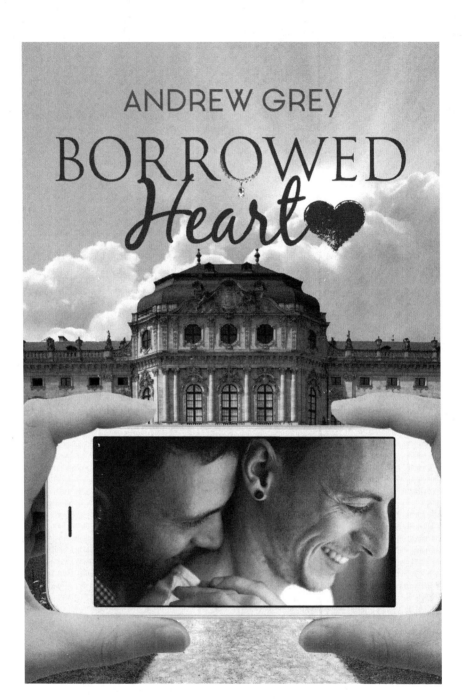

Robin, the recipient of a brand-new heart, knows he can't give it to just anyone....

Robin's been through his share of upsets recently, from heart transplant surgery to a brutal breakup. But his experiences have taught him life is short, and he's ready to seize the day and start anew. A job at Euro Pride Tours is just the kind of adventure he's looking for. He gets to see the world and live a little, but love isn't on his radar screen. He isn't sure his heart can endure that again.

Johan might've disappointed his family by striking out on his own, but when he meets Robin, he has no intention of letting him down. Each man is just what the other needs to feel whole again, and while Johan might not be the man Robin originally thought he was, he's exactly what the doctor ordered to make Robin's borrowed heart beat faster. As the tour through Germany progresses, they grow closer, but when Robin's ex joins the tour, he could bring their blossoming love to a dramatic halt.

www.dreamspinnerpress.com

Martin Graham built his business from the ground up with hard work and intuition. Due to a degenerative eye disease, he's learned to rely on his other senses to feel out the competition. To realize his dream, he just needs to broker one last deal… and finally secure an assistant.

Brock Littleton is desperate for money—desperate enough take the job no one else wants: assistant to demanding, fussy, intensely private Mr. Graham.

Everything about Brock gets under Martin's skin in ways he never expected, making him realize a successful business isn't the only component to a happy future. But as Martin's deal comes together, one of the prices could be the relationship with Brock that Martin is just starting believe could be real.

www.dreamspinnerpress.com

Professional basketball player Bri Early needs a physical therapist after an injury, and he's heard that Obie is the best. Bri takes an immediate liking to the out-and-proud man with the magic touch, and even though Bri isn't openly gay himself, he'd never let anything stand in the way of something he wants.

Obie can't deny that the sexy athlete presses all his buttons, but he's a professional and has no intention of getting involved with a client. While they're working together, it's hands off, no matter how great the temptation.

But being a pro athlete isn't easy. Bri has enemies, and one of them is making his life hell. When his house is set ablaze, Bri can no longer pretend the threatening messages he's receiving are jokes. He needs a safe place to stay, and Obie can't turn his back. But the two of them in the same house is a recipe for combustion that could burn them both....

www.dreamspinnerpress.com

Reunited

CURSED

DREAMSPINNER PRESS

Andrew Grey

Back in high school, nobody noticed quiet nerd Kevin Howard.

But everybody noticed handsome, athletic, and ultrapopular jock Clay Northrup.

They had nothing in common and lived in different worlds.

But a lot can change in fifteen years, and when they meet again at their high school reunion, Clay is no longer the big man on campus, and Kevin isn't hiding in a corner anymore.

Can they put aside who they were? Can one night really lead to forever?

www.dreamspinnerpress.com

UNFAMILIAR WATERS

ANDREW GREY

With the pressures of the job bearing down on him, police officer Garrett Wreckley needs a vacation—in fact, he isn't given a choice in the matter. Since the water has always soothed Garrett's soul, he heads to the Caribbean, hoping some time alone sailing on the open water will help him pull himself together.

But even though he's taking a break from law enforcement, Garrett can't get rid of his cop's instinct so easily.

He meets Nigel, a young man as innocent as he is beautiful, who grew up sheltered from the world, exploring the beaches and tropical forests with only the company of his aunt, his brother, and the wildlife and sea creatures he befriended.

As sweet, passionate love blooms, their time in paradise feels too good to be true… and Garrett's gut and training tell him that might be the case. As he investigates, he quickly realizes everything is not as it seems. Will his snooping destroy not only their romance, but everything Nigel believes about his life?

www.dreamspinnerpress.com